COLLARDS & CAULDRONS

A Southern Charms Cozy Mystery

BELLA FALLS

Evermore Press

ISBN-13: 978-1072250487

Cover by Victoria Cooper

❋ Created with Vellum

Also by Bella Falls

A Southern Charms Cozy Mystery Series

Moonshine & Magic: Book 1

Lemonade & Love Potions (Southern Charms Cozy Short)

Fried Chicken & Fangs: Book 2

Sweet Tea & Spells: Book 3

Barbecue & Brooms: Book 4

Collards & Cauldrons: Book 5

Cornbread & Crossroads: Book 6 (Coming Soon)

*All audiobooks available are narrated by the wonderful and talented Johanna Parker

For a FREE exclusive copy of the prequel Chess Pie & Choices, sign up for my newsletter!

https://dl.bookfunnel.com/opbg5ghpyb

Share recipes, talk about Southern Charms and all things cozy mysteries, and connect with me by joining my reader group Southern Charms Cozy Companions!

https://www.facebook.com/groups/southerncharmscozycompanions/

CONTENTS

Preface   ix

Chapter 1   1
Chapter 2   13
Chapter 3   30
Chapter 4   49
Chapter 5   64
Chapter 6   77
Chapter 7   92
Chapter 8   104
Chapter 9   114
Chapter 10   125
Chapter 11   138
Chapter 12   149
Chapter 13   158
Chapter 14   169
Chapter 15   183
Chapter 16   192
Chapter 17   201
Chapter 18   210
Chapter 19   222
Chapter 20   233
Chapter 21   242
Chapter 22   251
Chapter 23   261
Epilogue   273

Southern Charms Cozy Mystery Series   283

Southern Relics Cozy Mysteries   285

Acknowledgments   287

About the Author   289

As a child of adoption, family is a big deal to me. I always knew how special it was that I was chosen to become a part of mine, which is kind of the idea I've added to my Southern Charms Cozy Mystery series. Nana's motto comes from the love I have for my own family.

This book is dedicated to the real Steve, Patty Lou, Matt, and TJ.

Preface

Charleston, SC and the area around it is a special place in the South. The food is incredible, the views spectacular, and I'm pretty sure there's some definite magic running through it all.

Most of the places mentioned are real, even if some of the names have been changed. I hope you get a real feel for how much the area means to me and how fun it was for me to go there to do research!

Chapter One

I might be a little biased, but I would swear to anybody the pretty baby in front of me must be the cutest in the entire world. Stroking her hair, I stared back at her big eyes looking up at me. Even if time stopped, I would always care for and love this little one.

"Who's a pretty girl? You are," I crooned, my fingers scratching the crown of her head and around the base of the diminutive bump of a horn. With my other hand, I held out a carrot.

The tiny unicorn took the treat with a gentle tug of her teeth and gnawed on it. TJ snickered as she finished her examination. With a grunt, she stood up from her crouched position and slung her stethoscope around her neck.

"You're spoiling her," my sister-in-law accused, her hands palpating down the small creature's body.

"Of course, I am. Who wouldn't? It's a freakin' baby unicorn!" My voice came out high and squeaky like the ecstatic little girl I was inside. "I wonder where her mama is?"

TJ blew out a breath and rubbed her already shrunken tummy. "I don't know. And this one seems to be doing fine on her own, although I'm glad we've already got a mare with a colt here. If we have to, we can set up kind of a foster mom for...what did we decide to call her?"

The young unicorn nudged my hand, sniffing it and searching for another treat. I scratched her muzzle instead. "We haven't. I kind of felt like since she appeared on the same day you had Charli Junior that my niece and goddaughter should have a say."

TJ sighed. "I told you we gave her the middle name Charlotte only because after you called her Junior so many times, we couldn't *not* give her your name. But her first name is still Rayline."

My mother's name. Every time I heard it, my heart got pulled in two, half a little sad at her absence and inability to hold her first granddaughter and half pleased that we now had our own new ray of sunshine in the family.

"I know," I gave in. "But she'll always be Junior to me."

"And she'll always look up to her Auntie Charli." TJ stepped aside so the unicorn could lie down to nap. She closed the wooden gate to the pen and joined me in staring at the tiny miracle.

"Traci Jo, we've got a real live unicorn living here," I exhaled in wonder.

TJ nodded. "I know. But I think if we wait until Junior...I mean Rayline is old enough to speak, this little one will go nameless far too long."

What did one name a unicorn when, up until the night of my niece's birth, I thought they were a pleasant myth? We had a legendary creature living in the old barn on my property with the other horses. Names were too important to take the task of giving one lightly.

"Are y'all still starin' at the poor thing? Why don't you leave it alone, Birdy?" My brother's voice cut through our reverent silence.

"Because she's cute," I countered, slapping Matt's arm with the back of my hand without taking my eyes off the tired baby.

My brother playfully smacked me back without hesitation. "You'd think you'd be paying more attention to your niece."

"I pay plenty of attention to Junior," I replied, using my nickname to rile up my brother. "Speaking of, if you're both in here, then who has Rayline?"

Matt ignored my question, caught up in marveling at the unicorn. When I repeated my inquiry, it takes a nudge of my shoulder for him to respond. "Hmm, what? Oh, Beau's watching over her. You know, for an old vampire, he's pretty adept at being a babysitter. We might have to call on his services if I'm ever gonna have a chance at alone time with my wife."

"Hey, you aren't your baby's main source of food. I can't be away from Rayline too long. I should go back to the house."

TJ's words trailed off when the little unicorn rustled in her straw bed and twitched her iridescent tail. "I should also call Caro Whitaker and make sure I'm doing everything right by this little one."

At the mention of one of the Red Ridge sisters, my stomach flipped. Even after two months, my goodbye to Dash still affected me. Although I could call him anytime using my spell phone, I wanted to give him space.

Oh, who was I kidding? I needed the space out of fear of so many things. With everything going on in Honeysuckle, from the grand entrance of my niece *and* a baby unicorn to my attempts to reconnect with Mason, I didn't need a reason to run to a man who was still engaged, thanks to a blood pact he'd made.

"Beau told me I'd find you out here." The detective's voice echoed off the wooden walls of the barn and bounced off my heart. The sunlight beaming through the barn's entrance silhouetted his athletic frame.

My stomach flipped again for a whole different reason, and I gripped the wooden gate and focused my eyes on the unicorn instead of the man who used to love me. But Mason no longer possessed the memories of those feelings.

I'd heard from Nana that Rita Ryder had died from complications of cancer while in warden custody. After everything she'd done, including ripping the memories of me from Mason's mind, I knew not one person walking this Earth would hold a parting party for that nasty witch.

Mason clapped Matt on the back in a manly greeting and

smiled at TJ. I received a curt dip of his chin while his eyes darted away from mine.

The detective cleared his throat and glanced down at the stall floor. "Wow, I still can't believe my what I'm seeing even though I'm looking right at it. A real live unicorn." He whistled low.

"I guess when something's in front of you, it's easier to believe." I winced from the unintended sharpness of my words. "She's living proof that miracles can happen."

While a unicorn living in my barn was beyond amazing, if I could have any wish come true, I'd want to rewind time and stop Rita a few seconds earlier. Stop her from stripping me out of Mason's mind. Cling to whatever had been blooming between Mason and me with everything I had in me. But none of what happened was his fault. Being mad at him all the time because of the changes in our relationship didn't help.

TJ stepped away from the stall. "I should be getting back to Rayline since I'm providing her lunch. Come on, Daddy."

I scrunched my nose. "Eww, could you not call him that in front of me? It's weird."

"But I am one now," Matt protested.

"And if your wife wants to call you that in private, that's y'all's business." I curled my upper lip for emphasis.

Mason chuckled, and it warmed my heart, melting away a little of my icy anger directed at him. I wished with all my might I could do something else to earn that sound again.

My brother pushed away from the stall, oblivious to the joke. "We've got a bet going as to whether or not Rayline will say Mommy or Daddy first. So, we've gotten into the habit of calling each other by those names."

"And yet, I don't see hide nor hair of your blessed daughter here." With dramatic emphasis, I strained to look for their baby.

My brother pinched me under my arm, making me squeal. "You're such a brat. Come on, *Mommy*, let's go feed our daughter."

Dread built in my gut. They wouldn't leave me alone with Mason, would they?

"You say that like you have any part to play in the process," my sister-in-law teased with a little exasperation. She patted me on the shoulder and gave me a look that conveyed her silent question if I'd be okay.

Chewing on my lip, I glanced at Mason who leaned over the gate, staring at the unicorn. In the past couple of months, I'd attempted to reconnect with the detective in small ways. Meeting him for coffee at the Harvest Moon Cafe with our mutual friends. Joining everyone for a picnic under the Founders' tree. Too afraid to be alone with him, I'd always made sure others were around in case he felt uncomfortable. Or maybe I was placating my own discomfort.

I gave a quick nod of reassurance to my sister-in-law and watched my brother and her playfully bicker on their way back to my house. One of the horses snorted and shuffled around in its stall. Birds nesting in the roof tittered and flew around the beams, their wings flapping rapid beats.

The head of my orange kitty Peaches popped up from

between a few bales of hay. She hopped up on one of them, yawning and stretching. With a little chirping purr, she bounced down from her perch and trotted over to me. Her little fuzzy head rubbed against my leg and then the detective's.

I reached down and plucked her up. "What've you been doing out here, Peachy Poo? Are you keeping the mice away from our newest tenant?" Scratching her behind the ears earned me a strong rumbling purr.

"I'll bet she's good at mousing." Mason's deep voice reverberated right through me.

"She's tiny but fierce. I'm pretty sure she could take on a dragon and win, if not by her claws and fangs then by her sheer cuteness. Isn't that right, Princess Peaches Yum Yum Fuzzy Pants." I buried my face into her fur to avoid looking at the detective.

"Such a big name for such a little thing." He reached out to pet my cat but waited for me to give him permission.

I took a step closer so he could reach her, and his fingers stroked the fur on her head. She closed her eyes in enjoyment, and for a brief moment, tendrils of jealousy gripped me.

Mason didn't follow up with anything else, and only the typical barn noises interrupted our awkward silence. He stopped petting my cat when she squirmed in my arms to be let down. With regret, I let go of my one buffer between the detective and me. Peaches bounded away after some tiny prey, and I leaned on the wooden gate again. My body hummed with the close proximity of Mason's presence.

"So," he started and stopped, rubbing the back of his neck.

For some reason, his similar discomfort put me at ease. "So," I exhaled with a slight smile.

He opened and closed his mouth a couple of times, still unable to look me in the eye. With a slight gesture of his hand, he waved at the sleeping baby in front of us. "So, a unicorn. Pretty amazing, isn't it?"

"Yep." My brain shuffled around the options of what I could say next, but everything seemed too trivial. The harder I tried, the dumber my ideas got.

Mason blew out a long breath and clasped his hands together. "Listen, Charli, I know things between us are..."

"Tense?" I offered up the truth because we both deserved that.

He snorted. "Yeah. And I know you've been mad at me because I haven't called you or really talked to you one on one. Until now."

My eyes jerked to his. "I'm not mad." I recognized the lie once it left my mouth.

He finally met my gaze, and the sadness pooling in his eyes crushed me. "I might not know you as well as you know me yet. But remember, I'm a detective. It's my job to read people. You've been angry at me for a while now." He held up his hand to stop my protest. "And you have good reasons. I understand we used to have something between us. A lot of people have told me, and I swear, I've been trying my hardest to remember."

I glanced down, willing the tears burning in my eyes not to drop. "I know you're working hard. And it's not fair for me to expect too much from you."

His warm hand covered mine. "You've been great, actually. You haven't pushed me. You always make sure I've got friendly backup in case I'm uncomfortable. I can tell you're a special person." He squeezed once and let me go. "But if you're waiting for me to regain my feelings for you, I'm afraid you're going to be disappointed."

The absence of his touch burned, and I reached out to regain the physical connection, grasping his hand in mine. "You couldn't disappoint me." I stepped closer and willed him to believe me.

Mason responded with a light brush of his thumb over my skin. "I can't undo what's been done. Even with the help of some of the strongest psychics we both know, they can't return what's not there. And I know that hurts you, which is the last thing I want to do to you, Charli." His voice ended on a strained rasp.

He was ending things between us. Closing the door on my efforts to return us to where we'd been. Dash had said I could save Mason. Looked like I was going to fail in my mission.

"I understand," I muttered, letting go of his hand. "I'll leave you alone. I hope you have a good life, Mason." In utter despair, I turned to walk away from him.

"Stop, that's not what I meant."

My feet refused to obey his command, although I slowed my pace. "What else is there for us?"

"It doesn't have to be the end of us. Why can't it be a new beginning?" he called out after me.

I continued to trudge away but with shorter steps. "I don't know what that means."

"How about you not leave and stay here to finish our conversation?" Mason rushed forward and grasped both of my shoulders, stopping me and twisting my body around to face him. "For goodness sakes, stop being so stubborn, woman. It's just so...so..."

I couldn't keep the corner of my mouth from curling up, but I did stop myself from mentioning how that had always been the way between us. "Fine. I'm listening." I crossed my arms, digging my fingernails into the palms of my hands to distract myself from the heightened awareness of his softened touch still on my shoulders.

The detective glanced down as he held onto me. His brow furrowed, but whatever thought frustrated him, he dismissed it and let me go. "I think we need to give up on trying to recover the past and see what we can do about the present. In other words, let's start over. I'm Mason." He stuck out his hand to shake mine.

It was an ending, at least to my attempts to fix what Rita had managed to destroy. A part of me would always mourn what we had before, but maybe there could be hope for us if we left the past behind like he suggested.

I accepted his offer to shake on a new start. "Charli Goodwin. Stubborn witch."

Mason chuckled and pumped his hand up and down. "I

should say it's nice to meet you, but I think we're a little beyond basic greetings."

"You think?" My snark earned a genuine smile, and I internally high-fived myself.

"I can tell you're gonna be an interesting friend to get to know better," the detective admitted.

"Friend," I breathed out. "I guess I can live with that. Plus, Alison Kate did pair us up in her wedding party."

Mason snorted. "Yeah, all your friends seem to conspire to keep us together." He bumped my shoulder with his.

I nudged him back, ignoring the skipped beat of my heart. "It doesn't have to mean anything more than you escorting me down the aisle. I mean, after Ali Kat and Lee get married, not that we'd be getting hitched or anything. Pixie poop." Clamping a hand over my mouth, I squeezed my eyes shut in an attempt to ignore the awkwardness.

Mason's hearty laugh interrupted my horror. He took my hand in his again, giving me the courage to stop internally cursing my tongue. A slow smile crept across my face and I joined him with hopeful chuckles.

"It'll be my pleasure to be the one to escort you." He squeezed me once and let me go. I flexed my fingers at the absence of his touch.

Movement from the little unicorn's stall interrupted our moment, and we approached the tiny beasty quietly. The creature snorted and blinked her sleepy eyes. Spotting the two of us, she rose on her four legs and shook her body from mane to tail. She approached with careful steps and stuck her head out close enough for us to touch.

Mason and I scratched her wherever she demanded, our fingers bumping into each other.

"Who knows," the detective said with a grin. "If miracles like this little one exist, then there might be hope for us yet."

Chapter Two

The sun shone bright the morning after Alison Kate and Lee's wedding. I should be at the day-after wedding brunch being thrown by Blythe at the Wilkins' house by the water, watching the newlyweds open their gifts. Instead, my impatient behind occupied one of the chairs on my porch while I listened to the creak of the wood underneath me while rocking my sleepy niece back and forth.

"It was a great wedding," I spoke in a whisper. "The bride wore a beautiful gown that made her look like a modern-day princess. The groom was at a loss for words for the first time in his life."

Rayline blinked her eyes as if she understood. I ran a finger down her downy soft cheek.

"After they were married, we ate some good food and danced up a storm. You know who's a really good dancer?

Your daddy. That's because our daddy, your grandpa, taught him." I didn't stop the moisture gathering in my eyelashes. "Dad said a man should know how so he can surprise his woman at any time, and they can dance through life together. My mom, your grandma and namesake, loved to dance."

A tear rolled down my cheek at the memories of random moments Dad would hum a tune off key, grab Mom, and swing her around the floor until she lost her breath giggling. The baby grabbed onto my finger with her tiny digits and squeezed, bringing me back to the here and now.

I lifted her up and kissed her bald head, breathing in her signature sweet smell. "You come from a long line of love, Sunshine."

Speaking of men who could dance, someone had spent time teaching Mason a step or two as well. Although we were paired together in the wedding party, we'd been distantly polite and friendly for the entire event. When it came time for the bridal party to join the new husband and wife on the dance floor, I expected a basic sway to the music. Instead, Mason had taken control, leading me around the floor with masterful ease, not allowing me to trip or fall at any moment. I'd told him it wasn't fair for us to outshine the newlyweds.

My body hummed to life on the porch, remembering the words he'd whispered into my ear. "They'll have the rest of their lives to shine. This moment belongs to us."

For a brief second in the universe, nothing else had existed, and hope settled again in my chest. But when the music stopped, our bubble popped and the polite awkwardness from before returned.

Rayline squirmed in my arms and squeaked in displeasure, mimicking my own mood.

"I don't know what will happen to us either, sweet girl." I picked up the binkie that had fallen out of her mouth and replaced it.

Before we settled back into our rocking rhythm, my fuzzy orange kitty jumped up on the arm of the chair and stared at the invader of her lap space.

"I'm sorry, Peachy Poo, your spot is currently taken. You're gonna have to learn to share." With my arms full, I couldn't even scratch her little head.

Nonplussed, Peaches sniffed around the bundle of baby. Satisfied for the moment, she stretched, digging her tiny claws into the flesh of my arm for good measure, and jumped to the rocking chair next to us. After turning a couple of times, she settled down to enjoy the warmth of the day and fulfill her role as my silent companion.

Voices floated across the field, and my heart rate quickened. I spotted Caro Whitaker walking with TJ after checking out our newest magical resident. The questions I'd wanted to ask her when she first arrived bubbled to the surface again, and I longed to run out there to confront her. But Rayline fussed when I fidgeted, so I forced myself to stay put and wait.

All three Whitaker sisters had accepted Alison Kate's insistent invites to attend, but they'd kept a polite distance and stuck to the edge of the party all night. Since my job as bridesmaid had to come first, I didn't get a chance to ask them anything.

The two professional animal healers walked toward me, deep in discussion about special care for the unique creature.

"Promise you'll keep me posted with any changes or observations," the eldest Whitaker sister insisted. "And thanks for the rare opportunity to see her."

My sister-in-law patted Caro on the shoulder. "I appreciate your insight on how to try and care for a being we all thought was mythical. Although I've heard you've worked with a hippogriff before."

Caro's steps faltered and her face hardened in surprise. "Uh, any stories you heard might have been greatly exaggerated. Besides, I told everyone involved to keep it quiet. If word gets out you're harboring creatures that might be legendary, you could end up fighting off undesirables, if you get my meaning."

"That's a good point," agreed TJ, rubbing her shrunken belly out of habit. "I might have to remind all of Honeysuckle to keep their mouths shut about our one-horned miracle."

Caro rubbed the back of her neck. "She may be young and still so small, but the magic inside her is astounding. It will be far more difficult for you to contain the secret when she comes of age. That much power roaming the Earth freely will attract attention."

"You can sense that in her?" TJ failed to hide her

apprehensive awe, walking up the porch steps to claim her daughter.

The newcomer swallowed hard, and her gaze flitted back and forth between my sister-in-law and me. "I don't normally reveal my magic to strangers." She blew out a breath. "But Ginny and Georgia told me you were good people, so I trust you."

"What goes on in Honeysuckle is our business," I said, holding Caro in my gaze. "We won't share what doesn't need to be said."

Her shoulders relaxed. "Sorry I'm so cautious. I should know better after all the stories I've been told. You didn't deserve my distrust."

"Let's get some sweet tea in you and then I'll take you to your sisters," TJ offered.

Too nervous to ask my questions, I got up from the chair. "You two sit out here and enjoy my porch. I'll get the drinks."

In the kitchen, I battled over whether or not I should ask about Dash. We'd texted on our spell phones a few times, but only traded basic information. I prepped three glasses with ice and pulled the pitcher of sweet tea out of the refrigerator, going back over all the scenarios in my head of what he meant when he always replied he was fine.

"He misses you," Caro's voice interrupted my thought-filled fog.

"Frosted fairy wings, you startled me," I exclaimed, placing a hand over my beating heart to contain it.

She grabbed a towel from the oven handle and knelt down

to wipe up some spilled tea. "I didn't mean to scare you. Just wanted to let you know. I'm surprised you haven't asked any of us about him."

I focused on pouring the drinks. "I've been a bit busy." The half-truth barely convinced me.

Caro finished and crumpled the damp fabric in her hands. "My sisters have told me about the progress with the detective. I guess he's decided to stop trying to regain his memories. That's gotta be tough on you."

My pursed lips held back nothing but silence. What words could express the limbo status I found myself in every morning I opened my eyes to a new day?

She regarded me with care. "My sisters and I discussed how much we should tell you and what was his to tell you himself. He's healthy. It turns out he's a pretty good leader and things are getting better with his pack."

I nodded, keeping my eyes trained on the floor.

"His brother Davis is living on my property," she continued. "Dash visits often, and we share meals once in a while. But honestly, he doesn't say much of anything."

I scoffed and took the towel from her. "He never does."

"Listen, I don't know what he is to you. But he's a friend, and I think he needs time to adjust to his life. And that's really all I feel comfortable in sharing. I'm sorry." Caro touched my arm in genuine sympathy.

I handed her a glass to take outside. "No, I understand. We've both got spell phones we can use to communicate." I paused to consider her last statement. "And frankly, I need time, too."

Caro's eyes brightened. "Phew. I thought you might try to hex me or something. Sometimes my siblings hate it when I try to play big sister to everybody around me."

"I've got an older brother, and I totally get it." I ushered her out of the kitchen and back to the porch. "If he asks about me when you return, tell him my number hasn't changed."

She laughed in approval. "Good idea, although he won't like that answer. And when will you call his number?" she challenged.

Until I fulfilled what Dash told me I was going to do and saved Mason, I couldn't do more than text him. "Soon," I lied and chose a line of deflection. "Are you and your sisters going to the witches' conference in Charleston?"

Caro raised her eyebrow but didn't push. "No. I heard about it from a couple of the guests at the wedding, but we won't be attending."

"Why not?" I asked. "You'd be more than welcome. And you can hang out with us."

She shook her head as she waited for me to open the door to the porch. "Thanks, but not this time. We're in the process of repairing our lives in the mountains after the Red Ridge battle. My sisters have been inspired by Honeysuckle Hollow and have some ideas that will take time to develop. But you guys have fun hobnobbing with the hoity toity. Definitely keep us in the loop."

THE BUS our group rode on to go to the conference bounced underneath my seat. I stared out the window on our way to Charleston but hardly noticed any of the scenery. My seat mate Blythe poked me with her finger again and again until I squirmed and swatted her away.

"Cut that out," I grumbled.

"No, you cut it out." My best friend leaned in so she could speak in a lower tone. "The cloud hanging over your head is gonna cause rain to fall on all of us if you don't stop moping."

I snorted and watched vast stretches of ploughed farmland pass as we drove by. "You know I can't conjure weather magic or any kind of specialized powers for that matter."

"Oh, boohoo, poor you. Yes, you somehow lost your tracking powers. And one of the guys you liked is obliged to get married sometime this year while the other one had his memories of you stolen so he no longer loves you." Blythe stopped short of listing anything else. "You know what? That's a lot to deal with. Who am I to tell you to stop being depressed?"

My friend's undying support shook me out of my mood. I leaned my head onto Blythe's shoulder and rested it there. "Thanks, B."

She stroked my hair, her touch sending ripples of comfort through me. "It's my job to be there for you. But I'll admit, it's been a little tough lately. And besides, it looked like things between you and the detective weren't horrible at the reception. I saw the two of you dancing together."

I leaned away from her and scanned the heads of the people sitting in front of us. Somewhere up there was Mason, so close and yet so far away.

"Maybe the two of you could take this time to get to know each other better in the here and now." Blythe bumped my knee with hers. "Based on the way he looked at you during the ceremony and the way he held you on the dance floor, I doubt the door between you is closed yet."

"What are you, a psychic now?" I teased. I wanted to keep Mason's and my mutual agreement not to dwell on the past and to move forward between the two of us.

She gestured at a seat diagonal from us. "No, but I know two who are becoming well-trained."

I watched Lily and Lavender deep in a private conversation. Except their mouths weren't open. "Yeah, their grandmother is pushing them hard. I'll bet Linsey's gonna be really jealous when she gets back from college. All her journalism know-how to get to the bottom of things won't hold a candle to her kin's abilities."

The bus drove over a bridge that spanned a short distance over water. Trees dripping with Spanish moss lined the shores and colorful sea grass rose in tufts in the water. The beauty of the Lowcountry tugged at my wounded soul and forced me not to dwell in my dark thoughts too long.

"It really is beautiful down here. We don't even live that

far away, but it feels like we've entered a new territory." I straightened in my seat to get a better look out the window.

"Eveline secretly owns a residence somewhere South of Broad Street she rents out to tourists for extra income. She invited me to use it, but since we're all staying at the hotel for the conference, I wanted to stick with my girls." Blythe held up her fist for me to bump.

I obliged, and we both giggled at our silliness. Alison Kate leaned over the back of our seat. "What's amusing the two of you?"

"You," I said, shaking my head. "Why in the world aren't you on your honeymoon, Ali Kat?"

Lee joined his new spouse staring down at us. "Because my wife didn't want to miss out on the event. We'll split off from everyone after the conference. I've reserved a place for us out on Wadmalaw Island. Only shrimpers and cicadas out there. I'll have my wife all to myself for an entire week."

Alison Kate blushed. "I love hearing you say that."

"What, that I get you all to myself?" Lee grinned like a fool who'd won the lottery.

"No, whenever you say *my wife*. Y'all, I'm married." Our jubilant friend shoved her left hand between Blythe and me, showing off the golden band that joined the other ring with a fat diamond on it.

"Yes, you are, Ali Kat. We're so happy for you two." The truth lightened my mood, and we oohed and ahhed over the photographs Lee had on his updated spell phone. Even Lily and Lavender risked getting out of their seat to crowd around.

"When is the new line of phones coming out?" I asked.

Lee pushed his glasses up his nose. "I've got my team on it. The more complicated the technology, the harder it is to get the spellcasting right. Also, the bigger mistakes we can make. I brought this prototype with me to see how it would work in a city like Charleston."

"Y'all need to sit down back there," Nana admonished from the front of the bus.

"Yes, ma'am," I called out, hiding my snicker behind my hand.

My grandmother whipped her head around to glare at me. "That better not be sassin' I hear coming from you, Charlotte Vivian Goodwin."

Whistles, giggles, and a general, "Ooh," rose in the air. I sunk down, my cheeks flaming.

"I hate when she middle names me," I muttered.

Blythe snickered, and I smacked her. The rest of the bus ride to the city saw very little drama or more middle-naming. We passed roadside stalls with seagrass baskets of all sizes and shapes hanging on display with ladies ensconced under umbrellas, weaving new creations. I could hear Lee taking pictures with his phone, increasing the number he took when we reached the big expansion bridge that led into the city.

I read the plaque about the bridge out loud. "'Dedicated to the Ravenel family for their long service to Charleston.' Hey, I wonder if that's the same family name as that guy who attempted to railroad Nana?"

"Pshh. He didn't get as far as he wanted to," Blythe

uttered. "Guess he learned what we all know. Never mess with your grandmother."

"Amen," I agreed and chuckled when a few other Honeysuckle residents echoed the same word.

The bus veered right off the exit to the historical center of the city. Old houses and buildings surrounded us the further we drove. Crowds of tourists roamed the streets, and a bit of worry settled in my gut. Since we lived in Honeysuckle, we didn't interact with a lot of mortals. It had taken me a while to get used to walking around those who had no clue about the magical world that existed when I took my year trip away from Honeysuckle. Needing reassurances, I squeezed Blythe's hand as the bus made slow progress.

"That's the market," I pointed out the left side. "After we check in, I might go there to shop for a gift to give to Abigail when I meet her."

"I still can't believe you invited her to come to the conference," Blythe noted. "I'm guessing you weren't ready to have her in Honeysuckle?"

I nodded in silent affirmation. The bus turned right onto Queen Street and slowed to a stop in front of a big tan building with elaborately crafted wrought iron work surrounding its balconies.

Nana stood up at the front and faced us. "Y'all might be wondering why I signed us up to attend an all-witches' conference, especially here. While I get your hesitation, I think it's appropriate that we show how strong we are by not being intimidated by the Charleston faction. That being said, y'all better mind your *P's and Q's* or you'll answer to me."

My grandmother flashed her scary stare over the entire group and Blythe shivered. "I'll never not be affected when she looks at us like that. Even when I'm old and wrinkly."

"Nah, she'll be long gone by then," I teased.

My friend shook her head. "Don't you know? Strong witches like her never grow old. She'll probably outlast us all."

The bus door opened with a hiss and a young lady wearing a crisp white blouse with cherries printed on it, a pink cardigan tied with purpose around her neck, and a leafy green skirt stepped onboard. A pink and green headband held her blonde hair back.

She clasped a clipboard to her chest and flashed a bright, perfect smile. "Welcome to Charleston and our annual conference. My name is Haywood Pinkney, and I'll be your point person today." Her eyes roamed over all of us until they landed on the seat Mason had taken when he boarded. "Be sure to come see me anytime."

A slight rumble rose in my throat, and Blythe jabbed her elbow into my side. "What are you, a shifter now? Quit growling."

I hadn't even noticed the feral noise had been coming from me. But the more she addressed the detective directly, the more I believed my fingernails could grow into claws.

"Even though you're a tad bit earlier than we expected, your rooms are already available," she continued. "Once you have your room keys, come to the other side of the lobby and check into the conference. You'll be receiving a nifty gift bag with a printed program of events and some local goodies. Tonight, you're on your own, but tomorrow we'll have an opening brunch in the hotel restaurant before the panels start. I hope to see all of y'all there." She flashed a flirty glance at Mason one last time and left the bus.

I mocked her last statement, repeating it in a funny voice. "What kind of name is Haywood for a girl?" I mumbled under my breath.

"Jealousy doesn't look good on you, Charli," Blythe admonished. "Let's get to our room."

I wanted to protest and tell my friend I wasn't jealous. But when Mason stood up with a cocky grin plastered on his face, I couldn't deny the heat of disapproval rising in me.

"I can't be jealous of what ain't mine," I admitted to no one in particular. .

Blythe volunteered to get the room key for all four of us while Lily and Lavender waited with me at the long tables with volunteers sitting behind them to check into the conference.

When I got to the front, an older lady smiled up at me. "Hey there and welcome. What's your name?"

"Charli Goodwin," I replied, watching her flip through the names in alphabetical order.

"Here it is." She pulled out a badge on the end of a lanyard. "Oh, you're from Honeysuckle Hollow."

"How'd you know that?" I asked, trying to look at what

she held to figure out if something was written on it. "Iola," I added, reading her own name tag.

"Uh, no reason. I guess I heard it from someone that y'all were here." She thrust the badge at me and forced herself to grin. "You can get discounts off of the hotel restaurants and bars if you show it to them. Wear it at all times during the conference, please. Here's your gift bag as well."

Accepting the full tote bag, I appreciated how it changed colors from light blue to a dark purple. I guess it made sense to have magical items at a witches' conference.

A bellhop helped us get all of our bags up to our two-queen bed room. He used Blythe's card to let us in. We jabbered in excited small talk as we looked around the room and claimed beds.

I went to give the young man a tip and the tote bag still hanging around my wrist switched from purple to bright yellow. Panicked, I fumbled to find a good explanation for a regular human.

"Don't worry, miss. The Carlyle Hotel is used strictly for visitors like you." He winked at me, and I noticed the wrinkles around his eyes for the first time.

David, based on his name tag, wasn't as young as he appeared. For a brief moment, his hair turned green and hung a little longer about his face. Recognizing his true nature, I appreciated his willingness to let the glamour go.

"You're a witch?" I whispered.

A slight frown on his lips alerted me. "No, miss. My

mother was a brownie and my father was a dryad. I got my mom's size though."

I glanced at the color of his hair. "Why the disguise? I like the green."

He blushed in response. "The management doesn't like us to show our...differences to the guests. Since I work directly with those like you, I'm required to maintain a glamour at all times."

"If you're part dryad, why are you working in the city? I thought most of your father's line would want to be closer to nature," I mused. When his cheeks and ears turned a brighter pink, I regretted my curious questioning. "Never mind."

"No, it's fine." He looked behind him up and down the hotel corridor. Leaning in so only I could hear, he whispered, "You might find that not everything will be as you expected here." Voices at the end of the hall alerted him, and he moved away from me, his glamour shimmering back into place and the verdant hue of his locks fading back to a dull brown. He held out his hand for the tip. "Thank you kindly, miss."

"You can call me Charli." I couldn't shake the sense that he had more to say. "I hope I see you again, David."

"Better not, Miss Charli. Enjoy your time here." He hurried off before I could ask him another question. The door closed with a thunk, and I returned to the chaos of my friends.

Once we unpacked all of our bags, we debated what we wanted to do with the little free time we had before the night's event. A knock on our door interrupted our list of possibilities. Blythe answered and invited the person in.

"It looks like four suitcases exploded in here," Nana sassed. "Where y'all gonna sleep?"

"Wherever us birds choose to nest," I answered back with an equal amount of feistiness.

My grandmother softened her glance. "Have you girls decided what you're doing next? If not, I'd like to go shopping at the market and visit some people I know. I thought it might be fun to spend some time with my favorite granddaughter."

"I'm your *only* granddaughter, Nana," I replied, eyeing her with suspicion. She only called me her favorite when she wanted something.

"Exactly. Let's go, girls," she crowed, exiting our room without waiting to see if we wanted to go with her.

I turned off the lights as we left, checking the locked door before following behind. I'd been sensing for weeks that Nana had something up her sleeve. Maybe today was the day she'd share. That prospect both thrilled and terrified me as we walked out of the hotel and onto the Charleston sidewalk.

Chapter Three

From the hotel, we walked past enormous houses with long porches hidden behind wrought iron gates bent in artistic curves and patterns. The market in the middle of the historic area consisted of several covered buildings with shops and vendors on both sides. Colorful goods invited us to buy and take them with us. If we weren't careful, we could spend an entire day and all of our money shopping.

I entered a local souvenir shop section and perused the different gifts while Lily and Lavender debated over some pastel-colored tins of tea from a tea plantation located on a nearby sea island. Would my cousin think tea was a good gift? Or maybe I should consider getting her a T-shirt to remember being here. But a shirt might be too small of a gift, plus I had no idea what size would fit her.

"You're thinkin' so hard, there's smoke comin' out of your ears." Nana tapped the side of my head. "What's goin' on up there?"

"Nothing," I replied with a frown. As much as I could use some comfort from the one person who meant the most to me, I couldn't burden her with issues about my supposed biological family member.

She opened up a crinkly cellophane bag of something green and offered me a taste. "Suit yourself."

I reached in and pulled out a dried okra. Crunching on its salty flavor, I allowed my grandmother to guide me away from my friends to another vendor selling beautiful jewelry.

"Perhaps you can get your cousin a simple necklace or bracelet." Nana fingered a silver chain with an ornate pendant that looked like some of the iron gates we'd passed.

I didn't even have to ask how she knew. Nana always knew. "But is jewelry too big of a gift? Like I'm trying to buy her approval or something?"

My grandmother kept eyeing the different pieces. "That's hard to say without knowing more about her or where she comes from. It can be hard enough to purchase a gift for someone you know, let alone a complete stranger."

I placed my hands on my hips. "Okay, spill it. You know more than you've said, don't you?"

She frowned once and cleared her throat, still not looking at me. "I know that when we did any investigation into her background, we came up with a lot of nothing."

The noise and bustle of the market disappeared as doubt

filtered through me. "You think it isn't a good idea to meet her?"

Nana's shoulders slumped and she blew out a breath. Worry mixed with a tinge of sadness swam in her eyes. "I don't know, Birdy. A part of me wishes she'd never contacted you. But that's the selfish part, and I think you have to take this opportunity to reach out and explore how you feel about things. Maybe get some of the questions you've had all your life answered. And I can't stand in the way of that."

She placed a warm hand on my cheek, and I struggled not to cry in such a public space. Sniffing a couple of times, I tried to tell her how much I loved her in one gaze.

"I know, Birdy, I know," she uttered. Taking my hand, she led me through the crowd and out of the first building.

The warm sun blinded me for a moment until we entered a second structure. Without stopping at any of the food stalls or to shop for other gifts, she led me to a vendor that featured bold bright pieces of art hanging on the walls and shelves full of stylized local items.

A young lady, wearing an African print yellow skirt and a red top with her hair in twisted braids covered by a yellow scarf, stepped out from behind the counter and greeted us. "Welcome to Gullah Gullah where we feature goods created by our community and artwork depicting our way of life. My name's Titia. Let me know if you have any questions."

"Is John D here today?" Nana asked, searching the area.

Titia's mouth dropped in surprise. "You know my grandfather?"

"Oh my, don't tell me you're little Letitia? Child, I remember you when you were itty bitty and crawling around our ankles. You've grown into a mighty fine woman." My grandmother beamed at the girl. "John D must be so proud."

"Yes, ma'am, I hope so," Titia gushed with pink cheeks. "And there he is, winding his way back to us." She pointed in the distance.

A man who towered over the crowd with his height held up two drinks to keep them from spilling. When he caught sight of Nana, his bright smile lit up the place.

"Vivi Goodwin, you are a beautiful work of art standing in the middle of my gallery. What are you doing here?" His voice boomed louder than the general din of the people, and his infectious cackle caused me to chuckle.

Nana fluttered her eyelashes in jest. "John D, you haven't lost a stitch of your charming ways. You still weaving your Lowcountry magic with your brush?" She opened her arms to accept his warm embrace after he handed the drinks to his granddaughter.

He gestured at the walls. "Been selling my work here for a couple of years now. Doing so well that we can feature some new Gullah artists. You looking for something in particular for your walls?"

It took me only a few seconds admiring the paintings to find one that called to me. "That looks just like our Founders' tree." I moved to stand in front of the large framed art.

"Ah, you found my latest treasure. That's one I've done recently of the Angel Oak out at the junction of Johns Island

and Wadmalaw. She's an old live oak that's got deeper roots than any inhabitants that have lived in the area. I took some liberties, leaving out the wooden supports for the biggest branches and all the tourists milling about," John D explained.

Nana settled next to me, inspecting the same piece. "I hope I can take our group out there so you can see it for yourself after the conference. In comparison, our tree looks like its younger sibling."

The artist had captured not only the image of the Angel Oak but also the energy of it. I swore if I put my hand on the canvas, it would pulse with magic.

"Don't touch it, Birdy," Nana admonished.

John D chuckled. "It calls to you, I can tell. And that there is just a lithograph of the original. It's a high-quality copy because I'm not sure I want to let go of the original yet. But if you like this piece, I'll give you a good price."

I could picture exactly where I'd hang it in the house. If I removed one of Tipper's older paintings that held no sentimental value for me out of the foyer and into another room, it could be one of the first things anybody saw when they entered my house.

Nana watched me with care. "We'll think on it for now. But my granddaughter Charli here needs to find a gift to give to someone who's an outsider to Southern culture."

"She belongs to you, Vivi? Well, bless, I didn't see the resemblance." John D pumped my hand up and down. "It's good to meet any kin of Vivi's."

I started to correct him as to why I didn't look like my

grandmother, but Nana spoke first. "You've met before, but she was a fair bit younger then."

The artist's eyes widened. "Now that you mention it, I do recall a few visits with your fine son and his family. Titia, that means you and Charli must have met before."

His granddaughter joined us. "I remember now. We used to make crowns out of dandelions and clovers while my brother James chased yours."

"And you liked to braid my hair," I recalled.

She grabbed my hand and squeezed it. "I still like playing with hair. That's my main job at a salon right outside the city. The other girl who helps run the shop couldn't come in today, so Grandpa called in a favor. On my day off."

"I used to change your diapers, so you owe me," teased John D. "Plus, you know your grandmama's gonna be happy to have you eat at her place for dinner. Vivi, why don't you and your crew come join us. You'd be more than welcome."

Nana considered the offer. "I don't know about all of us from Honeysuckle, but how about Charli and I join you? Will Mama Lee be there by chance?"

John D leaned back and rubbed his chin. "Well, don't that beat all. I wonder if she knew y'all would be here. If you want to see her, come with me."

Nana patted my arm. "You stay here and see if Titia can help you come up with a good gift for your cousin. Then come find me."

"We'll be on your right as soon as you exit the building,"

John D explained, holding out his hand for my grandmother to take. "This way, ma'am."

Titia giggled. "He's a handful on any day of the week. Now, tell me who you're shopping for and I'll see what we can come up with."

Blythe, Lily, and Lavender found me looking over all the products. I did my best to resist the pull of the Angel Oak painting, but it compelled me to look at it again and again. When Titia offered me the discounted price, I couldn't justify spending that kind of money on one object. A little disappointed, I let go of my desire to take the piece of art home with me.

The other girls bought some smaller trinkets from my newfound friend and I left with a Gullah cookbook written by Titia's grandmother, John D's wife Retta, and a small burlap bag of stone-ground grits in a bag. If Abigail wanted to get to know something about me, she could start with understanding Southern food like traditional shrimp and grits.

The rays of the sun blinded me again when I walked outside, but my ears picked up Nana's laughter. The four of us girls gathered around an older woman sitting underneath an umbrella weaving. On the tables in front of her, several different styles of baskets and containers waited for tourists to purchase. I picked up a wider flat piece to examine.

"That there's a fan-style sweetgrass basket. It was used to separate the chaff from the rice on the plantations out by the Ashley River," explained the lady, looking over her sunglasses at us. "When our people were stolen from the African shores, we brought our lives and skills with us and wove them into our survival."

I swallowed hard and nodded. "Yes, ma'am."

"Mama Lee, don't you remember my granddaughter Charli?" Nana asked.

The woman stopped working with her hands and gazed up at me from her chair. "The only Charli I remember was no taller than this here blade of bulrush." She held up the long green stem of the fiber she used.

"It's nice to see you again, Ms. Lee, and to reconnect with Titia." The more of the family I met, the more memories of my visits to the area popped in my head.

"Child, you can call me Mama Lee. Everybody does," she corrected. "And of course, I remember you and your grasshopper of a brother tearin' around the yard." She gazed up at my grandmother. "Is this the one?"

Nana nodded once, and my curiosity grew. "One what?" I asked.

John D cleared his throat. "Now's not the time, Mama. Maybe tonight after dinner."

The older woman resumed working the sweetgrass with her fingers while talking. "Y'all comin' to Retta's to eat? If you do, you won't go hungry for days."

Nana assured her we would be there. It struck me as odd that she didn't invite my friends to join us.

Mama Lee stopped working long enough to hand each of us girls a tan stemmed flower made out of knotted and curved natural fiber. "These here are palmetto roses made out of the fronds of our palm trees. They symbolize love and protection and will last if you take care of them."

We thanked her and asked her advice to find a refreshing drink. John D offered to escort us to a nearby cafe, but Mama Lee asked for me to stay behind.

My nerves kicked into gear as I watched my friends go, and Nana didn't offer me any clear explanation. Instead, she took the bag in my hand and nodded at the other woman.

Mama Lee stood up from her chair and held out her hands. "Come here to me, child."

Her fingers curled around mine, and I waited in silence while she stared at me through her sunglasses. She didn't say much of anything except a few grunts. Dropping my hands, she grasped my chin and turned my head in all different directions. It reminded me of Nana's inspection of me when my great-uncle Tipper accidentally cast a death curse on me.

"What do you think?" my grandmother asked.

Mama Lee placed her wrinkled palms against my cheeks. "Well, Vivi, my first thought is that this here pretty girl grew up into a beautiful woman." She gazed at me over her glasses and winked while chuckling low. "But yes, I think you might be right about her. I'll have my great-grandson bring in some of my medicines from Sol Legare when he comes to dinner."

I raised my hand, and both women stopped talking about me long enough for me to get in a word. "What are you talking about? What's wrong with me?"

Mama Lee patted my cheek and let me go. "Nothin's wrong with you that can't a little lovin' and some of my remedies fix. Now go enjoy the beautiful sunshine and see me tonight after we break bread together."

I walked away with Nana, confusion slowing my steps. "What's going on?"

"Remember when I told you that I'd consulted with some of my Gullah friends about finding your biological family before? Mama Lee is the matriarch of that family line, and I filled her in on some of your recent troubles," my grandmother admitted.

I stopped walking and waited for her to notice. She returned to me and I hissed in agitation, "Why are you telling people my business?"

Nana hooked her arm through mine and dragged me forward. "Because you're mine to protect, and I will invoke whatever help I can to protect you."

It took a great deal of effort not to yell at her. "And what help can Mama Lee provide?"

"This is the home of Hoodoo, Birdy." Nana's lips curled into a grin. "You might not remember learning about it when you were little, but tonight, you're gonna get to experience it firsthand."

⚬⚬⚬

I COULD HAVE FED myself for a week with all the food I ate at the Gullah Roots restaurant. Despite my head telling me not to stuff myself, I'd loaded my plate with a small portion of shrimp and grits, crispy fried goodies like chicken, catfish, and okra, and a helping of dirty rice. My stomach threatened to burst, but I still finished up the last of the ox tail stew over collards.

"Ms. Retta, I usually put a little vinegar over my collards, but yours are too delicious without that tang." I soaked up the last drop of pot likker with a piece of golden crumbly cornbread. "What type of meat do you use when you're cooking the greens down?"

Titia hung her head with a smile while a few of the other family members whistled. "You're gonna start an argument with that question."

"No, she won't because my lovin' husband ain't gonna talk out of turn since he wasn't the one she asked." Ms. Retta put a hand on John D's shoulder. "In my restaurant, we use smoked ham hocks with our collards. Now, my husband could talk the rest of the night how he thinks smoked turkey necks give a better flavor, but since your behinds are sittin' in my place of business, I think I'm the expert here."

The young man introduced to me as James, Titia's brother, cast a sly glance at his grandmother. "I agree with Pops. Turkey necks are better."

John D whooped with glee and leaned across the table to high-five his grandson. I watched the familial bickering with amusement and realized how much I wished Matt hadn't lost the coin toss between Mason and him to stay behind at the warden station. I'd have to text my brother tonight before I fell asleep and fill him and TJ in.

Mama Lee stared her great-grandson down. "I thought I

was training you better, boy. You might become a fine root healer, but you don't know nothin' about when to keep your mouth shut, especially when it comes to women."

"That's why he can't keep a girlfriend, Granny," joked Titia, earning her a punch in the arm from her brother.

Mama Lee pushed her chair away from the table. "They're gonna be all night with their foolishness." She patted me on my shoulder and walked toward the kitchen.

Nana and I followed behind her, pushing through the swinging door into the room full of hot stoves and bustling workers.

"Y'all clear out," our host commanded. Without saying a word, the kitchen staff turned off the burners, took dishes out of the oven, and left.

Mama Lee went over to a group of grocery bags sitting on a far counter. She dug through them with crinkling haste, pulling out items and placing them in order on the counter. Grabbing a mason jar full of clear liquid, she approached the stove and dumped the contents into a clean pot. Clicking on a burner, she left it to heat.

"Now," she started while still organizing, "this would be much better if you had the time to come visit me at my place on Mosquito Beach. But I see my great-grandson did bring me everything we need. Here, Vivi, I already had this prepared for you."

She handed Nana a bright red small pouch hanging from the end of a leather cord. My grandmother cradled it in her hand like a precious gemstone.

"Since you're determined to face the dragon head on, I made you a mojo bag of protection. In this flannel, I've placed a mercury dime, some High John the Conqueror root and Queen Elizabeth root powder, the needle I used to sew it up, and for good measure, some goofer dust. Wear it around your neck and against your skin, and it will offer you a shield of protection for as long as you're here," she instructed.

"What's goofer dust?" I asked, unsure if I wanted to know the answer.

Mama Lee hummed as she pinched a bunch of dried things from a small pouch and added them to the steaming liquid on the stove. "I come from a long line of healers and my husband was known as one of the area's most powerful root doctors. I keep jars of gathered dirt from where he's buried to use for extreme cases. Something dark shadows your grandmother's time here, so I added goofer dust collected before midnight. She will need some positive energy to protect her."

Nana didn't hesitate putting the necklace over her head and settling it against her chest underneath her shirt. "Thank you, Letitia."

The lady grunted once and busied herself pouring the contents of the pot into a mug. She brought the steaming drink back to us, taking out a small vial and pouring it into the mix. "Here, drink this down."

"Who, me?" I questioned, my full stomach knotting.

"Is there anyone else in this room who's had her power

stripped from her and lost not one but two loves?" Mama Lee challenged.

Nana rubbed my back for reassurance, shrugging her apology. "I figured you could use all the help you can get."

"Besides, child, it's just nettle tea sweetened with some honeysuckle syrup. I promise, you won't hate it." The kind sparkle in the older lady's eyes assuaged my fear.

I accepted the mug with a forced grin and a thank you. When I lifted it to my mouth, the familiar sweet scent calmed me further. Taking a small sip, I waited for something to happen. When nothing did, I worked on finishing the whole thing.

The experienced root healer took more items out and laid them in front of us. "The nettle tea does many things, but for your purposes, let's say it'll help protect your heart while its cleansed. Nettle's also good for breaking hexes and spells."

"I'm not hexed," I countered.

Mama Lee stopped what she was working on and faced me, one hand on her hip. "Maybe not by someone else, but you've done a number on yourself. You're so tangled up in your own grief and guilt that nothin's gonna break through without a little push. So, drink your tea while you stand here by me and listen."

Protests bubbled up inside of me, but they felt empty of truth. I had caused my situation and was having a hard time moving forward. In silent obedience, I opened myself to the possibility that maybe I needed more than just determination to fix my life.

"Your grandmother told me enough details to get me started, but I want to ask you a couple of things for clarity. You do have a void in you, which must be from givin' away your powers, even if it was for a good reason. Do you want them back? I can always help fill that void so it don't hurt no more, and you can live a more normal life with what you have right now." She held me in her gaze while she waited for my response.

The answer burst out of me. "Yes. Of course, I want my talents back." I still possessed basic magic, but losing my own powers made me realize how lucky I'd been to possess them in the first place. More than anything, I wanted them back.

"Okay. You may have times where you regret that decision, but I understand. My second question has to do with love, and I want you to think hard about your answer." She took my hand in hers. "Are you willing to accept someone into your life as your partner? No matter who that person ends up being?"

I concentrated on finishing the hot drink to give myself a moment to decide a question that had plagued me for months. If I could rewind time to have the two men in my life standing in front of me healthy and whole and have to make a decision, would I be able to choose? But that wasn't how life worked, and circumstances of our situations got in the way. Still, I didn't want to go through the rest of my life alone. I was brought up with people who loved others who supported them no matter what. I craved that above all else.

"I don't know who I would pick," I admitted. "But I still choose to love someone and be loved back."

Mama Lee's face relaxed into a big smile. "Good. That's a brave choice."

"I'm not brave," I uttered.

She squeezed my hand and let it go. "Love is very powerful, and choosing to wield its magic even for a short while takes courage. Now, we're goin' to put together your own mojo bag. I've got two lodestones here, male and female, to attract love to you as well as to strengthen the effectiveness of the work we do. Now these plants here might look like something you'd put into a stew, and maybe that's what we're doin'. Creatin' a stew of power just for you."

Goosebumps broke out over my skin at her willingness to help. "I truly appreciate you taking your time to do this, Mama Lee."

"Vivi has been a good friend. So much unlike her counterparts here in Charleston who treat us like we don't matter unless one of their kind gets desperate and comes to me to work the root for their needs. Only then do we exist in their eyes, yet they will never admit it." She gathered a bunch of the plants in her hand as she talked. "You come from an extraordinary family, Charli."

I glanced over my shoulder at my grandmother. My heart filled with absolute devotion to the woman who winked back at me.

Wiping a rogue tear away, I nodded. "I do."

"Now, pay attention. This is *abre camino* or road opener. Your stress about your situation has been blocking you from receiving anything. We gotta break you open. These are dried marigolds for love. I heard you've opened your own business. I'll add some bay leaves and sassafras to add to the luck in love, money, and success. A knot made from sweetgrass like I was usin' today will replace all negative energy with positive." Mama Lee placed all the items in the center of the fabric square before choosing a small vial full of blood red liquid. She popped it open and poured delicate droplets of its contents over all the items.

"What's that?" I asked.

"It's oil made from the St. John's Wort flower. When the yellow petals are soaked in the oil, it turns the liquid red. Although it can be used to boost your luck, like if you wanted to win money at gamblin', we're usin' it to help you break through and solve your blocked condition. I'll let you have the rest of this to take with you and charge your mojo bag after you leave. Now to sew it up."

She handed me a needle threaded with white thread and had me stitch the fabric together to make a pouch. Before I finished, Mama Lee took it back and finished it, sewing the fabric closed tight and tying it to a long leather cord.

"There." She cut the thread with her teeth. "Wear it as close to your heart as possible at all times. And take these bottles with you."

I accepted the bottle of St. John's Wort oil but held up the larger of the two. "What do I do with this one?"

Mama Lee cleaned up after us and put the items back in the grocery bags. "That's simple rose water. You can sprinkle it on your bedsheets or add it to a bath. I like to dab a little behind my ears and on my neck. The fellas won't be able to resist you." She wiggled her eyebrows at me while cackling.

"What do we owe you, Letitia?" Nana asked.

"Now, that hurts my heart, Vivi. You know your money ain't no good with me. We help whenever asked. I've requested your assistance in the past and you've come through. You asked now and I've given what I can. It's the flow of life between us, and I refuse to break it."

My grandmother sighed but didn't push. "The fact you think I need some help doesn't make me feel good."

Mama Lee stopped putting her stuff away and held my grandmother in her gaze. "You shouldn't. I'm no psychic, but you both have shadows hangin' over you. There are challenges comin' and it will take great strength to make it through into the light."

When Nana and I left the restaurant, we walked back to the hotel wrapped up in silent thoughts. It had grown dark, and I glanced into the large houses, wondering what my night would be like if I traded lives with whoever lived in them.

"I don't feel any different," I confessed to my grandmother.

She placed a hand over the place her mojo bag rested. "Hoodoo root work doesn't feel the same as what you're used to. In fact, it can be completely ineffectual unless you believe in it."

"Do you?" The question came out of a need for reassurance.

We arrived at the hotel entrance, and the light from inside

shone on her face. One of the hotel busboys opened a door for us, but Nana waved him off. "Letitia isn't wrong. I've felt it down to my bones that a challenge is brewing for me, and I've been concerned about you for a while." She cradled my chin again. "I believe in whatever help we can get, and I suggest you do the same."

Chapter Four

Even though the girls grilled me about what went on at the restaurant last night, I kept most of what Mama Lee had said and done a secret. A part of me still questioned whether or not to wear the pouch all the time. I couldn't understand how the individual items would combine to do anything other than get a little oily inside the pouch.

Before we went down for the welcome brunch, I grabbed the leather cord, slipping it over my head and placing the bag under my shirt. Spotting the taller bottle, I unscrewed the cap and blotted a little rose water behind my ears, on each side of my neck, and on the skin of my chest that dipped below the V of my neckline.

We joined the rest of our group from Honeysuckle once we got our plates of food from the buffet. The noise in the room rose from a dull buzz to loud cacophony of voices. I scanned the area, wondering if Abigail was seated somewhere in here.

I got up to get more juice and a deep voice interrupted me. "Where's your badge?"

"Am I under arrest, detective?" I turned to face Mason who stood closer to me than we'd been since our dance together at the wedding or before he lost his memories.

It took great effort not to swoon. My fingers itched to push back the little bit of curl in the front of his still-damp hair or to feel the bristle of the stubble on his cheeks.

"If I were going to place you under my hold, it would be for more serious infractions than not wearing your name tag this morning." The left corner of his lip curled up.

How long had it been since I'd seen this playful side of him? Swallowing my surprise, I chose to play the game. "Challenge accepted."

Thu-thump. Time stopped on a heartbeat. His eyes met mine, and a familiar warmth flooded my veins, melting my insides. *Thu-thump.* He said something, but his words were lost on me as I stared at his lips. *Thu-thump.* The scent of soap on his skin filled me up, and I forgot the past months of pain.

His warm hand touched my arm. "Did you hear anything I just said?"

"Hmm? What?" I cleared my throat and shook myself out of my momentary lapse. "Yes. No. Maybe?"

Mason chuckled. "Well, that's clear as mud. I was saying that you might want to go get your badge. I heard they're being sticklers about it to make sure that only registered attendants get into the panels."

"Plus, how else is Abigail going to find me?" I added.

His eyes widened. "Right. I forgot you were meeting her here. I think it's smart that you chose neutral ground for the first face-to-face."

"Spoken like a true warden," I teased. "But I wasn't ready to have her meet me in Honeysuckle." Worry and doubt coursed through me. "I wish Matt were here."

Mason's face dropped. "I'm sorry he didn't win the coin toss. If I had thought about it, I would have stayed behind."

"I didn't mean to make you feel bad. I can handle it." If I said the words, maybe they'd come true. My hand touched the mojo bag resting on my chest through my shirt.

His eyes flitted down and popped back up to mine, his cheeks reddening at getting caught like a kid with his hand in the cookie jar. "I'm learning that."

Mason's short statement reminded me that he wasn't the same person I used to know. I took a step back.

"Still, if you need back up, I'll be there for you. By the way," he leaned in even closer so only I could hear him, "you smell amazing." He winked at me and returned to his seat.

Confusion killed any appetite I had left. Just like that, the same guy I'd grown to care for returned in a simple promise and a flirtatious comment. How was I supposed to move forward when our crazy dance together whirled me around and around in circles?

Blythe promised to save me a seat for the first panel. I

barely managed to make it to our room and back before the presentation started, taking my seat in between my best friend and Clementine. My cousin greeted me with a warm smile and nudged Tucker to say hi, who leaned forward and offered me a weak nod.

"They sat down before I could tell them not to," whispered Blythe on my left. "Sorry."

I didn't mind sitting next to Clem. She and I continued to build on our burgeoning friendship, and after the dishonor her mother brought on herself with the Charleston witch council members, the poor girl needed as many friends as she could get.

Settling into my seat, I glanced around and wondered if Abigail occupied one of them. I tried to guess which person might be her until I caught sight of my grandmother.

Nana sat amongst the presenters at the front. She hadn't told me she was participating when we were together last night, and by the looks of her fidgeting body language, she wasn't too pleased to be there.

A lady with her nose poised in the air like she smelled something unpleasant stood up from her place at the end of the table and walked over and stood behind my grandmother. Her strand of pearls dipped forward as she leaned close to Nana's right ear. Whatever words were said through her perfectly plum-colored lips caused my grandmother to turn a bit pink and frown.

With an air of arrogant satisfaction, the woman straightened, ran her hand down her violet dress to smooth out invisible wrinkles, and clutched the strand of pearls surrounding her neck. She walked over to a nearby dais and tapped the microphone. Before she spoke, she scrutinized the audience. Taking a deep breath, she plastered a smile which held no friendliness.

"Hey, y'all," she drawled in an affected Southern accent. "I'd like to welcome you to our thirteenth annual conference for witches. For those who may not be familiar with me, and that should not be very many among us, my name is Priscilla Ravenel Legare, widow of the great Hunter Legare and mother to Peyton Ravenel Legare."

A smattering of applause from those who knew her peppered the air. She sniffed and waited until the rest of us joined in and clapped.

Blythe snorted. "When they audition for the role of wicked witch, she's a shoe in."

"And what's up with all the names?" I added.

Clem leaned in and whispered, "Tucker says they take their family lines very seriously. Even money can't buy you a spot in the upper elite circles. It's all about what bloodlines you come from."

"I know we have the tradition with the Founders' families and such, but that's...a whole other level." I tried my best to pay attention, but I couldn't help focusing on how much the direct bloodline of the family mattered here.

"Thank you," Priscilla continued. "We are so pleased to see our numbers more than double this year with witches from all up and down the coastal region. Y'all have come to our fair city to be inspired and learn more about how we can all share in how to maximize our magical effectiveness wherever we live.

"Now, today and tomorrow, you'll have a program of panels during the day from which you can choose to attend. Tonight is the big mixer held in the adjacent Hyperion Hall next door. Put on your best and your brightest, and let our local district show you a good time."

Panic clenched my gut. Based on what this lady wore for regular daytime garb, my go-to dress with sunflowers hadn't been my best choice to pack. Then again, Nana had told us to prepare one nice outfit, and being covered in my mother's favorite flower always gave me a boost.

"Please give a warm welcome to Frances Whitcomb, who will be moderating this first shorter panel to kick things off titled *Magical Communities: Who's In Charge.*" Priscilla lightly tapped her fingers against her left palm and took her seat at the end of the table.

"Thank you, Prissy. Let's dive right in," Frances began.

"Uh oh," I muttered, focusing on the title. "I wonder how friendly this discussion is going to be?"

The presentation started out with basic introductions and an overview of the magical life in each presenter's home base. Although both Nana and the other guest from a smaller Southern town answered with pleasant and positive details, Charleston's representative raised the glass of water sitting in front of her, taking a long sip to pause before she spoke.

When she finished her few swallows and with all eyes on

her, she sniffed once and clasped her hands together. "Well, that's all well and good for communities as small as yours, but in a town like Charleston, it is our job to police all of the magical beings as we have to co-exist with humans day in and day out. If we witches didn't take up the mantle, then who knows what kind of chaos could erupt?"

The moderator glanced at Priscilla and nodded once, looking down at her card full of questions. "I am sure both of the other towns full of witches have their own magical law enforcement. Can you elaborate on what you mean by policing, please, Prissy?"

"I'd be happy to," the three-named woman grinned.

"That wasn't a set up at all," snarked Blythe.

Priscilla looked out into the crowd with confidence. "You see, we were not the first settlers in this area when our descendants were granted land. It took us many generations to learn how to whip all the supernaturals into shape and bring about some form of order, especially the wilder fae."

Nana's reddening face matched my insides. "I don't like where this is going," I uttered in a voice loud enough for others around us to hear.

"Before World War II," Priscilla continued, "having any type of fae running around on their own could endanger the secrecy of our kind. It wasn't until afterward that our leader at the time figured out a way to allow the fae and their kind to live in a more civilized manner with some inspired foresight and ingenious spellcasting. Nowadays, the only problems we have within our community is deciding what outfit to wear to the next solstice gathering."

The woman dared to smile and expect applause for her explanation. The loudest claps came from the locals while the rest of us wore confused or bitter faces.

Watching my grandmother, I knew it was a short matter of time. "Three...two...one..." I counted.

The words burst out of Nana's mouth. "In what world is it acceptable to suppress another supernatural being's rights to live?"

The crook of Priscilla's mouth quirked up. "Before our kind rose up to take control of all magical enforcement, there were recorded accidents and yes, even deaths caused by those not of witch lineage. All beings in the world require some form of organization, and they respond best when there is someone in charge doling out rules and upholding them. You have your own form of government and control in your town, do you not, Vivian?"

"Yes, but we also allow any and all beings with magical powers to live with us. Even the unwanted ones," my grandmother declared with pride.

Her counterpart raised a perfectly-shaped eyebrow. "And yet, it is not always a harmonious place. Have you not had issues with a fairy who assisted a vampire in stealing from your citizens? Has a troll not been arrested on suspicion of murder?"

Some gasps and murmurs rose in the crowd in reaction.

"She's taking that out of context," I complained.

Nana sat forward in her chair. "Actually, evil comes in all guises. Witches have been some of the criminals who have been brought to justice for their actions. It's not what we are but who we are and how we choose to live our lives that make a difference."

Clem fidgeted beside me, and I watched her place a hand on Tucker's leg. Her husband and my former betrothed's face blanched, and I cringed, knowing that one of the criminals my grandmother spoke about had been his father.

"Yet, I know you can see the wisdom of having witches maintain the positions of control. In your council, you have had generations of the same families hold positions. It seems your ancestors may have been wiser than you." Priscilla paused to take a breath to make another point.

Nana jumped in. "I can't say we're perfect in Honeysuckle. Yes, for our own reasons, we have had witch families at the head of the town council. But recently, we held an election where anyone was invited to run. In the end, it was a gnome and our head of security who won the seat, and—"

"After there was a murder involved," interrupted Priscilla. "And the other candidate, a vampire, had been found in bed, so to speak, with the murderer. In terms of your enlightened election, there still remains a majority witch vote, unless my math fails me."

She held up a manicured finger to stop my grandmother from speaking, a dangerous move that could put her in dire jeopardy of being a target of Nana's expert hexing. "Here, we have very little problems with the other kinds. They accept our authority and act accordingly. I think we would all agree, when it comes to magic, order is far superior to chaos."

Frances had been watching the back and forth like a tennis match, her mouth gaping a bit. When an uncomfortable silence descended over the room, she cleared her throat and flipped through her cards. "Uh...umm...it seems we're running out of time. I'd like to ask the presenters to give any last thoughts on the subject."

The other small-town representative batted her eyes. "I guess I would say that it depends on who the citizens are where you live. But mainly, I think live and let live is the best policy."

Nana pursed her lips, ignoring the poignant gazes from the two women from Charleston, expecting her answer. When my grandmother refused to speak, Frances uttered a sound of pain when Priscilla's lower half hidden by the table jerked.

The poor lady gritted her teeth into a forced smile. "And you, Vivian? Any final thoughts?"

"I have thoughts, but they won't be final," Nana replied. "The idea that policing any other magical beings through the use of power wielded by our kind to suppress who they are and how they function should be investigated and revoked. Yes, each community has a right to act in their best interest, but that should be more inclusive, not exclusive."

I stood up, whooping loud and long while clapping until my hands hurt. Almost the entire crew from Honeysuckle joined me. Frances waited until we stopped and indicated for Priscilla to bring things to a close.

The wicked witch stood up, looking down at Nana. "Bless your heart, sugar, you are more than right. Each community should take care of its own. However, I do think that when one of them seems to be outperforming in every way, there might be something worthwhile to consider. Thankfully, all of us will leave with lots to think about long after this weekend is finished.

"I want to thank my fellow panel members for being so willing to share their points of view so freely. We'll take a fifteen-minute break before the next panels start in the adjoining rooms."

The room buzzed with nervous energy, and I crossed my arms. "If we thought the issues between Honeysuckle and Charleston were over, I think we were just schooled on how wrong we were."

Tucker frowned and stepped closer to me. "We should have been prepared for a presentation like this. I will make sure to have a word with Prissy after the panel."

"You know her?" I jerked my thumb toward the front of the room.

"I know of her," Tucker admitted. "She's been kind of the queen bee of the witch community at large in Charleston even before I attended college here. There were stories..." He whistled low but didn't finish. "I know her daughter. Peyton isn't bad, but you should see how her mother treats her."

Nana wasted no time leaving the front and pushing her

way through the crowd in my direction. She huddled with Tucker for a brief moment where he agreed to lodge a direct complaint to Priscilla on behalf of our town council. Without talking to anyone else, she grabbed me by the elbow and pulled me along with her.

I stumbled out into the main foyer of the hotel, fear coursing through me. My grandmother knew how to handle herself, and seeing her exhibit very heated emotions should make everyone move out of her way.

"That woman," Nana huffed. "It was all I could do not to bless *her* heart and hex her conceited hiney."

I pulled her further away from the crowds gathering outside the different conference rooms. "Why would she go on the clear offensive like that? It doesn't make sense to invite all of us down here and then basically insult everything our town stands for."

My grandmother drank down the rest of her water bottle in a few gulps. "I didn't see it coming. And Letitia was right." She touched an area over her torso, and I suspected she wanted to make sure her mojo bag was still there.

Curiosity got the better of me. "What did she say to you before everything started?"

Nana's gaze chilled me to my core. "She said, 'This is for my brother.'"

"Who's her brother?"

My grandmother closed her eyes. "Calhoun Ravenel."

Cold chills ran up my spine. "Oh no. Don't tell me he's here, too."

"No, thank goodness," Nana uttered. "I heard from the lady who ran the panel that he left to 'explore their family history in Europe' after he came home from Honeysuckle." She made quotation marks in the air with her fingers.

"You mean, he ran away to escape his humility." A long groan escaped my mouth, and I looked for the nearest exit. "So, the guy who got beat at his own game when he tried to take over Honeysuckle has a powerful sister. Well, let's leave. You'll have all of our support if we just get up and go."

"And let her get in the last word? Not on your life!" Nana's loud declaration echoed in the hall and a few heads turned to watch us. She lowered her voice. "I didn't come to Charleston looking for another fight, but I refuse to back down from one when it presents itself. If she wants to go to battle with me, then she can learn as well as her brother did that I won't stop until everything's finished. No, we are not leaving until either Priscilla or me isn't standing."

Worried about creating a spectacle, I escorted my grandmother away from the nosy observers and toward the hotel lobby. Seating her on a fluffy couch shielded by a large flower arrangement, I left her to cool down while I fetched another bottle of water.

"Excuse me, Miss Charli?" a voice called out.

I turned to find David chasing after me, waving a piece of paper in the air. He thrust it into my hand when he reached me.

"This message came through our front desk for you," he said. "Is everything okay? Do you need anything?"

An escape hatch? A door to the fairy path? Everything in me screamed we should leave, but there was no moving Nana when she'd made up her mind to stay.

"No. Priscilla whatever her other two names are kind of attacked my grandmother in the first panel. Except, if you didn't know the context, not everybody would know it was an attack." I shook my head. "We'll be fine."

David's eyes darted back and forth. "Be careful, miss. Once the great witch sets her focus on you, it won't be long until everything ends."

His words alarmed me, and I grabbed his arm. "What do you mean? And what did *she* mean when she talked about controlling the fae?"

Another hotel worker in uniform passed by, and David jerked out of my grip. "I can't say more. I need my job." He hurried off, leaving me to add his lack of explanations to my pile of concerns.

I returned to Nana's side and opened the folded paper, reading the message out loud. "Abigail was held up on her way here. She promises to meet me at the cocktail mixer tonight."

"That's good," uttered Nana, still lost in her recovery from the first panel.

"Is it?"

My doubt pulled my grandmother out of her frustrated thoughts. She sighed and rubbed my back. "It will be whatever you make of it, Birdy. Go in expecting the best. If things don't work out, you know that your family is here for you either way."

Family. That word seemed more loaded with high stakes than ever while we were outside the borders of our safe small town. At least now I knew when and where I would finally meet a member of my biological family. If bloodlines were so important in Charleston witch society, tonight, I would get a chance to find out exactly what kind of people the blood in my veins attached me to.

Chapter Five

✦

The rest of the panels for the day held no animosity or agenda. Nana insisted that our group from Honeysuckle show some solidarity and backbone by maintaining attendance. She acquiesced to letting me and my friends skip the catered lunch and go to a restaurant a few steps further down Queen Street to a restaurant that boasted thirty years of being voted as having the best she-crab soup. The tasty Lowcountry specialty soothed many jangled nerves as well as proved their award-winning claim deliciously valid.

After supper, Blythe and the two Blackwood cousins joined me in our room in getting ready for the mixer. Steam billowed out of the bathroom, erasing the wrinkles from our dresses while Lavender did the best she could in getting makeup on my face.

"I don't want to be all caked up," I complained.

Lavender dabbed a sponge underneath my eyes. "It's just powder, silly. And see if you can calm down. Your aura is all wobbly. We'll be with you when you meet Abigail."

I jumped when someone knocked on our door, and Lavender insisted I stay still unless I wanted eyeliner applied directly to my eyeball.

"Hey, girls. Who wants their hair done?" crowed Alison Kate.

"As I live and breathe, it's Mrs. Chalmers! How did you manage to get Lee to let you out of his sight?" teased Blythe.

Our friend blushed and looked away. "We haven't been that isolated from y'all."

"It's your honeymoon, Ali Kat." My friend's happiness radiated from her and seeped into me, clearing away some of the fog of nerves. "You're allowed to take some personal time when you choose to come to a conference first. Anyway, can you do that thing with my hair like you did for your wedding?"

With a little of her natural skills and a tiny bit of magical talent, Alison Kate brushed, teased, and sprayed my hair into a messy bun at the back of my neck with curled tendrils framing my face. Even if my dress wasn't that fancy, at least the rest of me could look the part.

"You'd best be getting your dresses on. The mixer will start here in a few minutes," Alison Kate declared after she'd finished with all of us. "I'm going to go back to our room to fetch Lee."

"See you tomorrow morning," Blythe teased from the bathroom.

I inspected my reflection in the mirror after I put on my dress, still worried that I wouldn't fit in. However, a glance at the bright yellow sunflowers against the black of the fabric reminded me to shine no matter what. And maybe my hair, makeup, high-heeled sandals, and an air of confidence would do the trick.

Another rough pounding on the door surprised the four of us. When Lily answered, Ben and Mason entered our room.

"It looks like a bomb went off in here," my advocate friend stated when he observed the chaos of necessary supplies to make us gorgeous scattered everywhere.

"I think it doesn't matter if the ends result in such beauty," added Mason.

"Detective, that sounds an awful lot like a compliment," Lavender teased. "And may I say that the two of you look snazzy in your suits."

Ben fussed with his tie. "Yeah, but I'll be dying to take this all off at the end of the night. It's a little too warm to wear so many stuffy clothes."

"Would you rather wear my dress?" Lily lifted an eyebrow at her beau. "I'm sure that can be arranged."

"Maybe later." Ben's cheeks turned pink and he winked at his girlfriend. "But for now, I'm here to escort you and your cousin to the mixer."

"And I have the honor to escort you and Blythe, Charli." Mason crooked both arms for us to take.

"Pfft. You go with Charli. I don't need anybody to

chaperone me anywhere." Blythe brushed past both men and out into the hall.

Mason turned his gaze to me. His eyes roamed up and down my body once. "That's a beautiful dress. Have you worn it before?" he asked.

It never came to mind that I'd brought the dress I'd worn the night he'd made me dinner and told me about his past. While the choice to wear it had more to do with the sunflowers and less to do with trying to recall a night that had changed things between us, it saddened me that he clearly didn't remember.

"I don't think so," I lied, looking down at the floor to avoid his gaze.

"Hmm. I could have sworn..." His brow furrowed for a brief moment until he shook it off. "Well, it looks lovely on you. Shall we?"

My hand flew to cover the spot over my heart when it seemed like he might remember our night. It occurred to me I wasn't wearing my mojo bag. However, I doubted it would add anything to my look, so I chose to leave it behind.

"Let's go." Wrapping my arm through his, I relished the warm strength his presence afforded, especially in the tense situation the mixer would certainly be.

Between meeting my biological cousin and trying to keep Nana from hexing the grand dame of the Charleston witch community, I definitely had my hands full.

ALTHOUGH WE PASSED a side entrance into the venue, the staff of the hotel requested we go outside and enter through the grand entrance on Meeting Street. A fence of tall iron bars with long spikes at the top wrapped around the large structure.

"Who do they think they're trying to keep out? Giants?" Blythe asked, cocking her head back to take in the gate.

We walked through an arch of decorative iron patterns and up the bank of stairs into the stone hallway. Once we entered, a double grand staircase weaved its way around the front hall. A general buzz of excitement spread through the crowd gathered on the first floor.

"I so did not wear the right thing," I admitted, noticing all the sparkles and fitted bodices surrounding us.

Mason leaned his body against mine. "I think you look better than any of these ladies. They're trying so hard to meet expectations that their hard work shows."

"And I'm just the easy-going country bumpkin, right?" I snorted.

Mason stopped guiding me through the groups of people and faced me. "No, that's not what I'm saying. I think you're beautiful whatever you wear. And that dress...I don't know, I just like it."

The desire that he'd said he liked *me* instead of the dress rose to the surface. Grabbing a glass of champagne from a nearby waiter, I took a couple of swallows to tamp down the notion.

"Is it hard for you to take a compliment? Or harder for

you that it comes from me?" Mason asked, not letting me escape.

I waited for the tickle of the bubbles to go down my throat before answering. "I don't know. I guess both." My cheeks heated, and I focused on the task of figuring out which woman in here could be Abigail rather than the complications of the man in front of me. "How am I supposed to identify my cousin if we've never met?"

We perambulated with slow steps, weaving in and out of the crowd. I tried to grab the attention of any young woman of the approximate right age and give a little nod of my head. Not one of them did more than offer me one in return or a polite but cold grin.

I backed into someone and apologized before even turning around. My grandmother's kind face deflated my worry. "Oh, thank goodness. Do you have any good ideas how I should find Abigail?"

"Name tags would come in handy now, wouldn't they?" Nana chuckled.

"Or having my talents back. If I could, I would use her note to me to try and make a connection." I furrowed my brow, trying to recall how my special magic even felt when I possessed it. The longer I didn't have it, the less I could remember.

Mason spoke from behind me, "Have you even tried?"

"And, what, be disappointed yet again?" I finished my glass of champagne and shook my head. "What's the point? I guess worst case scenario, I'll tap every girl on the shoulder and ask them their name."

A light and airy giggle interrupted us. "You can start with me. My name is Peyton, and I'm glad I found you before things officially started." She offered a manicured hand as if she were royalty and we were meant to kiss the sapphire ring sparkling on her finger.

"It's nice to meet you, Peyton," Nana replied. "May I ask why you were looking for us?"

The young lady batted her long dark eyelashes with coquettish ease. "I have someone here who needs to speak with you. Mama, will you join us, please?"

Priscilla excused herself from her current conversation and stood next to her daughter. The genuine smile on her face froze when she caught sight of Nana.

"Now, Peyton, I feel as if you have some scheme or another planned. You know we both have limited time for games tonight." Although Priscilla's eyes regarded my grandmother, she did her best not to address her directly.

"Mother, now, I told you how you behaved this morning was unladylike. And if there's anything you taught me, it was that women never get as far in life as respectable ladies. I think you owe this fine woman, who is our guest here in Charleston, an apology," pushed her daughter.

"Peyton Ravenel Legare," Priscilla exclaimed. After a moment of indignant reflection, she sighed and turned to speak to my grandmother. "I suppose after careful scrutiny that I may have been a tad bit...aggressive this morning.

What my brother did, he did of his own will and against my advisement. It has always been a bad habit of mine to defend him."

"Okay." Nana hardened her expression and waited.

"There now. Everything is smoothed over," Priscilla proclaimed.

Peyton placed a hand on her arm to stop her from moving away. "Mother, you didn't actually apologize."

"Didn't I?" Priscilla waited for someone to let her off the hook. When she felt the pressure of all our stares, she broke. "Oh, Peyton, you'll learn that we ladies understand when an apology is needed or not. And in this case, perhaps Vivian is strong enough to not need the actual words. If you will excuse me." Before finishing her statement, she sashayed away with a rustle of her formal dress.

Her daughter's face dropped in exasperation, and she ran after her mother. The two stopped at the side of the room and spoke in low voices until Priscilla pulled out of her daughter's grasp.

She erupted loud enough for her voice to reverberate off the walls. "Enough, Peyton. Not here." The older lady stomped up the stairs while her daughter followed behind, both ignoring the spectacle they had become.

"I think the daughter might be in trouble," Blythe guessed, chewing on an hors d'oeuvre of some sort.

Mason perked up. "Where'd you get the food?"

My friend made a show of eating the last bite with a sly grin. "You're a detective. Use those skills to find some."

He touched my arm. "I'll be right back."

I watched him walk away, the figure of his body inspiring more than just me to stare and admire. One elderly lady went out of her way to pinch his behind as he passed. He turned to see if I'd noticed, and when he caught me looking, he shrugged.

"You know, I think someone needs to talk to Priscilla. Maybe smooth things over before anything gets out of hand. You gonna be okay on your own, Birdy?" Nana checked.

I slipped my arm around Blythe's waist. "I've got backup. And when Mason returns, I'll have backup for my backup."

Straightening with determination, my grandmother slipped upstairs to confront the mother and daughter.

"There goes trouble," I admitted, a little worried but knowing that when Nana set out to do something, she did it. Anyone who stood in her way tended to get injured in her wake. Better to let her say what she needed to and be done with it.

Mason returned holding a plate filled with finger foods and three glasses of champagne. I caught that Hayden girl from earlier gawking at the detective. Narrowing my eyes at her, I placed my hand on his arm, rubbing it while I stared her down until she moved away.

"I really shouldn't, but I'm gonna." I accepted one of the glasses and raised it in victory of my tiny personal win. "If I have to play referee with Nana at the same time as having the most important meeting of my life, I better get a little loose."

"Try one of these shrimp puffs to help," suggested Blythe.

"Don't eat all his food," I chastised her while picking up one for myself.

Mason shrugged. "I brought enough to share." He held up his glass. "Here's to new connections."

"Amen," nodded my friend, clinking my glass. "You have to make eye contact or you'll be asking for bad luck."

I glanced at her while she clinked our glasses together again. Turning to do the same with Mason, I got caught in his gaze. So far, he'd been nothing but nice to me. Even walking a fine line as if somewhere inside of him, a part of him remembered where my place in his life had been. Confusion, awe, and something else I didn't recognize rested in his eyes.

"Cheers," I managed in a weak voice.

"To new connections," Mason repeated in a rumbly intimate tone. He downed the contents of his champagne flute in a few gulps. "Another?"

"Probably shouldn't." After finishing the second glass of the bubbly alcohol, the haziness of a buzz lightened my mood. "But we're away from home and should do away with shoulzz...I mean, shoulders. Nope. Shouldn'ts." A giggle escaped my lips, and I covered my mouth with my hand.

Something tickled against my left shoulder, and I brushed it off with my hand, perusing the plate of goodies for something tasty. The annoying feeling returned, and I tried to bat whatever tapped my shoulder away.

"Charli," Mason called out, looking at something behind me.

"What?" I turned around and found a slightly shorter young woman biting her lip and waiting to talk to me.

"Are you Charlotte Goodwin?" she asked.

My stomach clenched, and the buzz from the champagne fizzled from the adrenaline that shot through my veins. "Yes. But mostly people call me Charli."

She blew out a breath and smiled wide. I recognized her countenance of happiness. I'd seen something similar when looking in the mirror, although her hair was a few shades lighter than mine.

"Abigail?" I asked.

She nodded. "I don't know if this sounds weird, but we look like we're related. Should we hug or something? Or maybe it's too soon."

I enclosed her in my arms without hesitation. "In my family, we hug." Her body stiffened at the contact and I let her go.

"I'm sorry. That was nice. And I guess some families do embrace." She glanced at the floor in embarrassment.

"And some don't, like yours?" I clarified.

Before she could answer, a gong resounded throughout the hall. Priscilla walked to the balcony in the middle of the two grand staircases and waited for the rest of us to quiet down.

She held up a fluted glass in front of her. "Ladies and gentlemen, witches all, I welcome you again to our fair city of Charleston." Her voice broke on her last word, and she brushed her fingers against her throat while she coughed.

Taking a sip from her drink, she attempted to regain her poise. "Excuse me. Now, where was I?"

"You were welcoming everyone, Mother," Peyton called out from underneath the balcony.

"Looks like the daughter made it out alive," Blythe commented.

"What?" Abigail asked.

I leaned in to whisper, "I'll explain later."

Priscilla grasped the railing and attempted to continue. "As *cough* I was saying *cough cough.* You are all welcome..." She gasped for breath, glaring out with widened eyes.

Mason stepped forward. "I don't like the color of her face."

The woman's porcelain countenance morphed from pink to red to a deep purple in mere seconds. Murmurs of concern rumbled through the crowd. The detective burst into action, bounding up the stairs two at a time.

The glass in her hand fell to the floor and shattered, its contents dribbling over the side of the balcony. Priscilla clutched the pearls around her neck, scratching the skin. Her mouth moved, but no sound came out.

With a loud grunt of effort, she cried out in a rasp, "Peyton!"

Her body collapsed in a heap while her tight grasp broke the string of pearls, the small jewels scattering over the balcony and raining onto the floor.

Mason made it to her first, crouching down so I couldn't

see him. His voice rose above the din of concern. "Is there a doctor or a healer here?"

Nana appeared from behind and joined the detective on the balcony of the second floor. A group of women mobbed up the stairs to check on the status of their queen bee.

An unfamiliar touch on my arm jolted me and I turned my attention to Abigail. She watched the scene with morbid curiosity. "I don't understand what's happening."

Since I hadn't even had time for a proper introduction, I had no idea what her level of comfort around a crisis would be, and we really didn't have time at the moment to check. I kept my eyes glued on Mason, hoping he'd give me a sign of Priscilla's recovery.

When he glanced down at me, he shook his head once enough for me to comprehend.

"What's going on," I said, "is that rather than enjoying the beginning of a new connection, we're going to have to focus on the death of one instead."

Chapter Six

The roar of everyone talking at once deafened me. Once Priscilla didn't get back up, people speculated on what had happened. Although Mason wasn't a native warden, his experience from being on a bigger force up North assisted him in maintaining a level of control over the body until the local authorities showed up.

A commotion broke out when Peyton pushed her way through the nosiest of the onlookers at the top. She shrieked and wailed, trying to push the detective out of the way.

"Mother, no! You have to get up!" Tears ran down her cheeks and she dashed the back of her hand against her skin, smudging her makeup. Even disheveled, she mimicked her mother's perfection.

Mason motioned for a few closest to them to hold Peyton back against her profound protests.

One of the enormous wooden doors into the Hyperion Hall swung open with a groan, and a man wearing a suit walked in. "What's going on here," he yelled to be heard over the noise.

A few other wardens followed behind him, jumping into action and herding most of us out of the way. One of them pushed me back with the flat of his hand against my body without an apology, and I debated what kind of first impressions I would make if I cast an itty-bitty stinging hex his way. Abigail supported my arm to keep me from losing my balance, and I decided not to do anything to jeopardize her first impression of me.

The first warden stomped up the stairs and frowned down at Mason. "Who are you?"

Our detective spoke in a lower tone so the rest of us could only hear his murmured explanation. Whatever he said provoked the local warden, whose mustache twitched in disapproval.

"I don't give a good spell in Hades who you are or who you've worked with before. In Charleston, we run things, and this is *our* crime scene." He grabbed the lapel of Mason's suit to forcibly remove him.

Without Priscilla standing in front keeping everything in order, her community of witches scrambled to figure out what to do next. Frances, the moderator from the morning panel, stepped up to speak to the head warden, but no matter what she said or the hand gestures she used while speaking, his level of frustration grew.

"That's it!" he exploded. "Everybody shut up right now."

Reacting to his tone, a hesitant hush fell across the first floor of the hall.

The warden in charge barked out orders. "You, Jenkins, close the door and stand guard. The rest of you, we're invoking PAC-142 protocol. Nobody's leaving the scene until we have some answers. Call in for reinforcements to take positions outside the hall."

A general ruckus rose from the crowd, but I agreed. The only way to be sure of what happened would be to stop who came in or out. That meant staff or guest, we would all be in for a long night.

Relieved by the Charleston warden, Mason returned to stand with us. Others from Honeysuckle shuffled in our direction.

"So, what do you think is going on?" I pressed.

Mason's eyes kept flashing to the upstairs area. "It's hard to say. She seemed to choke on something based on what we saw before she collapsed. They need to place a warden's shield around the body and the immediate area to preserve the evidence." His hands curled into fists, and his frustration at being forbidden not to do his job rolled off him.

"How long will we be held in here?" Abigail asked.

Mason blinked at the newcomer until his busy brain caught up. "You must be Charli's cousin Abigail. I'm sorry this is the circumstances of your first meeting."

"It's fine," I replied out loud, attempting to reassure more than just myself. "It'll provide more time for us to get to know each other."

Mason ran his fingers through his hair, mussing it up. "My guess is the wardens will question everyone here and take statements. That could take a couple of hours at least." He reached out and brushed his hand against my arm. "Your grandmother's another story."

Not wanting Abigail to get too embroiled in things concerning my grandmother, I stepped away to speak to him for a tiny bit more privacy. "What do you mean?" I asked in a lower tone.

"I was busy trying to handle the situation when she appeared from the second floor behind us. Whatever happened up there, your grandmother was in the area." Mason attempted to convey some level of apology in his gaze, but I brushed it off.

"She wasn't the only one. Peyton followed her up there first." Tucker's words about the daughter and mother's relationship in years past came back to me, but he hadn't been a student at the college here for a while. Perhaps the personal dynamic of Peyton and Priscilla had changed, and I was barking up any possible tree that didn't point to Nana being involved.

"I'm sorry, Charli, but if the wardens do their job, Ms. Vivi should end up a pretty decent suspect. You need to prepare yourself for that very real possibility." His hand reached out to mine, but he pulled back at the last second. "I should go check with some of the wardens coming in and see if I can find out more before the chief shuts me down again."

My gang closed ranks around me, demanding to know everything Mason said. Before I revealed anything, I grilled each of them on what they saw. When I got to Abigail, I realized my blunder of jumping into the fray without her understanding why. I paused to formerly introduce her to my closest friends.

"How are you enjoying Charleston so far?" Blythe joked, indicating with her hands at the chaos around us.

Abigail blushed and shuffled her feet. "The trip into town showed me the area is full of a lot of beautiful things. I wasn't prepared for anything major to happen tonight though. Other than meeting Charli," she added quickly.

Alison Kate tore her attention away from Lee to help ask questions. "And where are you from?"

Abigail bit her lip. "Mainly up North, but I've lived here and there. I'm kind of a nomad of sorts. It's nice to visit new places though, so I don't mind."

Lavender pretended she needed to speak to her cousin, maneuvering around Abigail's back, her eyes narrowed on the space above the new girl's head.

Lily whispered something in Ben's ear, and he frowned. Shoving both hands in his pockets, he rocked back and forth on his heels. "When did your family become aware of Charli's existence?"

Abigail's breathing sped up, and she sputtered for a second. When she recovered, she wrung her hands and glanced up to her right. "There had been rumors getting back to us of a person with tracking talents in a small Southern town, but we only found out she was related to us very recently."

Lavender's brows knitted together. She shook her head and mouthed, "Lie."

Sensing the presence behind her, Abigail jerked away from my friend and hugged her arms around her body. A part of me wanted to protect her from the interrogation. But if Lavender was right, we needed to figure out what truths she was hiding.

Abigail focused on some activity on the second floor and she gasped for a brief second. Realizing her noise garnered her attention, she waved her hand in front of her face.

"I know you want to know more about me, just like I want to learn about you. But it's getting kind of stuffy in here. Do you think they'd find some chairs and let us sit down or bring us some drinks?" she suggested.

Agreeing with her ideas, I searched for a nearby warden. I found one making notes while she asked a couple I didn't recognize questions.

"Excuse me, ma'am," I interrupted with my best effort at politeness.

The young lady snorted. "Wait your turn. Someone will get with you soon enough."

"Actually," I challenged, "some of us were wondering if we might have chairs to sit in and some food and drink. It seems it's going to be a long night, and it will go better if we're not exhausted."

The warden curled her top lip at me. "Are you kidding me? A very prominent witch from our city has dropped dead, and you demand to have a place to sit down and eat a meal?"

The husband of the couple spoke up. "I think she might be right. Let us all eat a little something and you might maintain better control of the situation."

"And these heels are killing my feet. A place to sit would be wonderful," his wife agreed.

The young lady stared at the couple she was interrogating. "Let's finish going through my questions and I'll see what I can do, Mr. and Mrs. Tradd."

"Thank you, Deputy Howard. Your efforts will be duly noted." The man straightened his tailored suit jacket and smoothed out his tie.

When the couple finished their interview, the young warden hurried off. I thanked them for helping me out.

"Your ideas had merit, and it seemed she needed a little push. Thank you." The husband dismissed me with his cold ending to our conversation. I'd bet all the money sitting in my wallet he was a local and used three names as well.

It took more than a half an hour for our situation to change. Eventually, someone organized the wardens to bring out chairs and allow the catering staff to circulate the food they had already made. It ran out before we got any, but at least someone had found a huge stash of water bottles so we all had something to drink other than alcohol.

Since there weren't enough chairs for everybody, my friends and I took turns sitting while we waited. When a warden no older than Zeke back at home approached us, we all stood up and waited our turns.

He wrote down all of our names and asked us questions about what we'd seen. None of our stories varied, and the warden's lack of reaction suggested we recalled the same thing everyone else did.

The young man flipped through his small pad of notes. "And can any of you confirm that an elderly lady showed up on the second floor after Ms. Ravenel Legare collapsed?"

My friends regarded me with care. It wouldn't do any of us any good to lie. In fact, it could do more harm to the goodwill our little group from Honeysuckle still had.

"Yes, the *older* lady, not elderly," I corrected, "was my grandmother. She had gone upstairs to talk to Prissy, I mean, Ms. Legare. Since she sits in the high seat of our town council, she'd be a good person to have around in a crisis."

"Ma'am, her presence is something to be questioned, not praised. I'll have to put this on the official list to investigate." He scratched the side of his head with the eraser of his pencil. "That's all for now. You'll be informed soon of the next steps."

Soon in his world of time did not match my expectations. Another couple of hours passed, and every attendee wilted around the room. People like Abigail and me shared seats while others like Blythe threatened to sit on top of us.

"Ladies and gentlemen, may I have your attention," the first warden on the scene called out. "I'm Chief Huxley, and I will be in charge of this investigation. At this point, all of you should have been interviewed as you all have been witnesses to the untimely death of Priscilla Ravenel Legare."

"Do they have to repeat her full name every time they speak about her?" I asked under my breath.

The chief warden continued. "We will be lifting the ward from the Hyperion Hall here shortly. I understand that we have many people attending the conference from out of town staying at the hotel. Please file out quickly and quietly and return to your rooms.

"I understand that there may be a large amount of confusion, and at this time, we are not prepared to make a statement. Until we are, everyone should expect to remain here until our medical examiner gets a shot at the bod—er, Ms. Ravenel Legare."

Someone from the back of the room and another witch community spoke up. "Are we all under arrest?"

"Certainly not," clarified Chief Huxley. "However, until we have more details, I need all of you to stay where we can find you."

The husband of the couple I'd met earlier stepped forward. "What if we're not staying at the hotel?"

The chief gave a curt nod of respect to the speaker. "I will make an exception for those of you, like Mr. William Aiken Tradd, who are from the area. Please return to your homes, but do not leave the immediate vicinity until otherwise notified."

I watched some silent exchange of agreement pass between the two of them. Why did the chief have to ask the other man's permission? A pit opened in my stomach, and I wished I could go back in time and stop us from coming to the conference.

Instead of exiting through the two large doors of the front of the hall, wardens and hotel staff escorted us through a side entrance that led directly into the building where are rooms were. While some of our group who had rooms on the second floor walked up the stairs, my girls and I waited to ride the elevators to the upper floor.

"I can't wait to see what happens next," proclaimed Abigail. "I hope your grandmother is okay."

The chief held Nana back while insisting everybody leave. No matter what they could throw at her, I knew the old broad could handle herself. That didn't stop my need to stand as a shield in front of her.

"Me, too," I admitted.

Abigail got off one floor below my room. "I guess I'll see you tomorrow morning. Despite what's happened tonight, I'm glad we're finally meeting."

Remembering Lavender's discovery, I hesitated to reply, and the elevator doors shut. While we trekked to our room, none of us made a peep. We waited until we were within the privacy of our room before anyone spoke.

"Well, I know I said sometime today that Ms. Prissy Pants should be brought down a rung or too off her ladder of control, but I didn't anticipate what happened," Blythe said, taking off her earrings.

"Did Mason tell you anything that might give us a bigger

clue as to what went on?" Lily asked as she sat down on the edge of her bed.

My brain worked too hard to try and solve our predicament for me to hear my friend's question, asking her to repeat it again before answering. "No, he said he would ask the other wardens questions until he was told to stop. And he disappeared for the rest of the night."

Lavender huffed and placed a hand on her hip. "Now that we're alone, I just have to say that I'm not sure I like Abigail. She was definitely lying while we talked to her."

"Interrogated her, you mean. Anyone being peppered with questions as hard as you guys were asking might get a little flustered." I didn't understand why I defended someone I'd just met other than a weak sense of familial solidarity.

"Oh, you wanted to know as much as we did. Besides, since my powers have been trained up, I can tell she's using a lot of energy to hide something. You should proceed with caution, my friend," warned Lily.

I chewed on my thumbnail. "Maybe. Or maybe she was nervous. I don't know." With a loud groan, I lifted the hotel quilt and crumpled onto the bed face first, pulling the cover over me. If I ignored everything and stayed underneath, maybe all my troubles would disappear.

Blythe peeled back the heavy fabric. "Come on. Let's get you changed out of your dress, wash your makeup off, and put you to bed. I think we could all use some rest."

While my friends managed to fall asleep fast, I stared into the darkness of the room. Turning onto my right side, I listened to Blythe's rhythmic light snore to ignore the *what if's* and worry over what happened to Nana. At some point, my eyes shut and my mind drifted off.

A loud repeated pounding startled me back awake, and my heart almost leaped out of my chest. In my hurry to get to the door, I stubbed my toe and swore out loud.

Blythe clicked on her bedside lamp. "What's going on?"

"I don't know," I admitted, checking the peephole. "It's Mason."

He rushed inside and closed the door behind him. "The chief is declaring that Priscilla was murdered. The entire place, including the Hyperion Hall and all of us guests, are under warden house arrest. They've warded everything. We can't get out."

My chest heaved in panic. "What does that mean? They can't keep us under lockdown without cause." Our room changed from luxuriously large to far too cramped in an instant, and claustrophobic dizziness struck me.

"Steady now." Mason caught me by my arm. "Let's sit you down somewhere."

He moved me out of the entrance and to the edge of the bed. All of us girls sat in alarmed silence, waiting for the standing detective to give us more information.

"They can keep the wards up for as long as the chief deems necessary, but I don't imagine they'll do it for long. The hotel won't like it, but it will also hurt the magical community of the town's reputation if they don't hurry up and find the killer." The way Mason glanced at me sent frigid chills across my entire body.

The wardens needed someone to blame for the murder. I asked the question I dreaded the answer to. "What does that mean for Nana?"

Pity shadowed his face. "They took her to the warden station and will be holding her until the morning at least. Charli, my instincts tell me you need to prepare for the worst. This is a very tight community, and they are going to protect their own."

My brain exploded with a thousand things I should do at that exact second. "Where's my spell phone? I need to call Matt. He has to know. Where did I put it? Should we hire a local advocate or get Jedidiah up here. No, wait, Ben's here. But I really need to call Matt or he'll be mad at me."

I found my phone and scrolled through my contacts. Dash's name popped up, and I opened the last text that he'd sent while we were in the first panel. "*I'm fine. U ok?*"

My fingers hovered over the keys to type back how far from okay I was and to beg him to come to Charleston. If my world was falling apart, then I needed all of my friends there. Even the wolf shifter. I slumped onto the edge of the bed.

Blythe came over and put her arm around me. The gesture of comfort almost broke the fragile emotional dam holding back my torrent of tears. "Calm down. Let's take this one step at a time. Go ahead and make your call."

"It won't work," Mason declared. "The wards have blocked

all devices from functioning. We can't even text each other, which is why I came to you directly."

Anger snuffed out my fear. "So, what? We're supposed to sit here and let them railroad my grandmother and not be able to do anything?"

If it took everything I had—the rest of my magic, my actual blood, or even my life—I would make sure Nana would make it home again.

"In theory, yes." The detective rubbed the back of his neck. "At least, that's what they hope will happen. Thing is, they have no idea who they're messing with."

Lily scooted to the edge of her seat. "I hope that means you've got a plan hatching in that head of yours."

Mason tapped his lip with his finger. "Not a plan so much as knowing what assets we have that they won't take into account. For example, Ben used his advocate status to protect your grandmother and provide her with immediate representation."

"That's *my* man," Lily cheered.

"And Lee is all over the spell phone issue, testing out ways to bypass the wards," the detective explained.

"But you're a warden," Lavender stated. "Aren't you supposed to be against the breaking of the law?"

"Again, in theory. But there's something not right about how the whole situation is being handled." Mason's voice took on the authoritative tone of his job. "And if they're going to corrupt the law, then I can turn a blind eye to someone trying to bend the rules."

I'd stayed silent, trying to listen in on everything being said despite my growing dread. "That's it?" I croaked out. "That's the plan? Hope Ben can keep Nana from being arrested for something she didn't do and put our faith in Lee to get our spell phones working? And for what? So, we can call home and tell them we lost the best leader the town has ever had?" My bottom lip quivered, and large tears flowed down my cheek.

Mason crouched down in front of me. "Of course, that's not it. I'm going to call on the biggest asset of all." He wiped the wetness from my face with his fingers.

I sniffed. "What's that?"

"You."

Chapter Seven

✦❦✦

Sleep eluded all of us until early morning. Mason had promised he would come get me as soon as Nana was released and allowed to return to the hotel. Hunger and the natural alarm clocks of our stomachs woke us after only a few hours of restless sleep.

As I dressed for the day, I found the mojo bag underneath a pile of clothes still strewn about on the floor from getting ready for the event last night. Slipping the leather strand over my head, I vowed to keep it on for the rest of our time here.

Unsure how the hotel would run under a wardens' lockdown, we made our way to the same dining area we'd eaten at the day before. Guests hovered around every available table talking in low tones. The words "murder" and "Honeysuckle" were spoken more than once.

Everybody sat in sections based on where they had come

from. All of the witches from our town were in the back corner, isolated from the rest. We waded through the crowd to make it to them.

Lily and Lavender's grandmother, Mimsy, got up to give me her seat. I protested, but Blythe pushed me to take it. My friends treated me with kid gloves, fetching me coffee and a little toast, which was all my stomach could handle. Mason, Lee, and Ben were nowhere to be seen.

"I took Lee a little breakfast to eat in our room. When he gets on a roll, he doesn't like to be disturbed," explained Alison Kate. She hugged me around my shoulders. "I'm so sorry for everything."

Others offered their apologies as well. Their comfort ought to make me feel better. Instead, my frustration grew. Tired of being coddled, I banged my hand on the table and stood up. The whole dining area grew quiet, and I realized my mistake.

Slinking back into my chair, I took a couple of deep breaths. I leaned forward and spoke only loud enough for our group to hear me. "Listen, if there's anything we know, it's that my grandmother is tougher than nails. What she needs is for us to stay alert and aware. Listen in on as many conversations as possible. Gather what information you can and bring it back to me or Mason."

"Ooh, I was wondering if this would push you two back into your old ways," exclaimed Ms. Mimsy with a little too much glee.

Everyone understood the high stakes and agreed to do

what they could to help. I tried to give them assurances, but I couldn't manage to make a smile reach my lips.

Once I ate a little and let the coffee kick in, I became restless to do something, anything, but I didn't have a clue where to start.

"Have you seen your cousin?" Blythe asked, while munching on a muffin she snatched before the hotel staff put away the food.

In all of the commotion, I'd forgotten about Abigail. "No, did you notice her in here? I don't even know what room she's staying in, only that it's a floor below us."

"What are you going to do about her? I mean, if you trust what Lavender said, she seems to be hiding something from you," my friend pressed.

I pushed back from the table and stood. When we navigated around the other tables, I kept my gaze straight in front of me instead of confronting all of the stares aimed at my back. "I don't know. I mean, we're basically strangers, and I hadn't intended on starting out any kind of relationship with her by saying, 'Hi, cousin, are you lying to me?'"

"I get that." Blythe turned around and shot a nasty look at all the onlookers behind us. "Nosy witches. Whatever happened to polite Southern ignorance? They could at least wait until we'd completely left the room before talking about us."

"For all they know, my grandmother committed a murder last night. Their suspicions make them forget their manners," I guessed.

I really didn't know what to do about my cousin. She was a problem I needed to solve at a different time, but thanks to being stuck in the hotel, I'd have to confront her at some point.

Mason and I spotted each other down the long hall at the same time, and I almost broke into a full run to get to him. By the time I reached him, I'd run out of breath from sheer anxiety.

"They're escorting her inside right now," he explained, taking my hand and dragging me behind his wide strides.

The two of us made it to the lobby where the young lady warden, who'd given me a hard time about chairs and food the night before, held the door open for her boss to walk my grandmother inside. Ben followed behind, the stern expression on his face scaring me. I moved to rush forward and throw my arms around Nana, but Mason squeezed my hand and held me back.

"Ms. Goodwin," the chief announced in a voice louder than necessary, "You are instructed to stay here until you are either cleared of any wrongdoing or you are arrested. Is that clear?"

Nana maintained a blank appearance, not giving the man in charge the satisfaction of upsetting her. "Yes, sir," she replied with zero emotion.

Frustrated, the chief motioned for the other warden to step up. Ben came forward and observed while the young man placed a device around her ankle. It clanked shut with a flourish of his fingers.

The chief crossed his arms. "This device will make sure you comply with my order."

He put hands on both of my grandmother's shoulders and turned her around. With a little force, he walked her toward the front doors until she emitted an audible gasp.

"That's out of line, Chief," Ben warned.

"As you can see," the chief continued, "your boundaries are well-defined."

I strained against Mason, who squeezed me even tighter until his grip stung. "Let him finish and leave," he insisted.

"I understand," Nana agreed. "And I will be available to talk to any warden or detective you put on the case, Chief Huxley."

The head warden raised an eyebrow. "Of course, you will. Until then, I would advise you to stay out of sight. No telling how you'll be treated when everyone knows you're the murderer."

"Thinks, not knows, right Chief?" I corrected, unable to hold back anymore. "My grandmother is innocent until you prove her guilty."

A smug satisfaction flooded his eyes once I gave him the reaction he craved. "We'll see." With too much enjoyment, he stroked his mustache and waited until the last second before exiting the hotel with his wardens.

I opened my arms to finally embrace Nana, but she shook her head. "Not here. Let's go somewhere else, but not my room. I'll bet they've cast some bugs of some sort to listen in there."

"We could go to my room. The girls will leave if you need them to," I suggested. "Unless they've spellcasted bugs in there, too?"

"It's entirely possible. How about my room?" Mason asked, checking with Ben over our heads. "They'd be less likely to mess with a fellow warden and advocate's space."

The four of us took the elevator up to their floor in tense silence. My eyes darted around the tiny space, looking for anything out of the ordinary that might indicate someone was spying on us. When the doors opened, Mason put out his arm to hold us back, ducking his head out to survey the hallway. Satisfied, he ushered us into his room.

The door shut behind us and Nana's shoulders slumped. She groaned as she sat down in a nearby chair. Mason went to the bathroom and came out with a glass of water for her. She drank it down in a couple of gulps.

"Thank you, Detective," she uttered, holding it out for him to take and refill a couple more times. Once she quenched her immediate thirst, she finally looked at me and opened her arms.

I threw myself at her, kneeling at her feet and laying my head in her lap. Most of the tears I'd managed to hold back burst out of me as I sobbed like a child. The thought of possibly losing her from the ridiculous circumstances had affected me more than I'd realized.

Her hands stroked my hair, and she muttered soothing words, trying to get me to calm down. Once my sobs turned to dry hiccups, I glanced up at her.

Tears streamed down her face, and for the first time, I saw cracks in her strength and vulnerability mixing with her courage. I wanted her to tell me everything would be okay and work out, but it occurred to me that maybe I had to be the one to carry the Goodwin strength for both of us.

Ben held out a box of tissue, and I took one, wiping away my tears and blowing snot into it. "So ladylike," I joked.

Nana scoffed. "I think politeness goes out the door when you're almost arrested. Speaking of, you did a good job in there, Advocate." She offered a weak smile to Ben.

My friend's cheeks turned a little pink at the compliment. "They definitely didn't expect you to have such immediate representation, and if they had been more organized, they might have attempted to keep me out. As it was, I'm glad I was there to keep them from getting out of line with their questioning."

"Is it as bad as I cautioned you it might be?" Mason pushed off the wall he'd been leaning on and came over to sit on the edge of the bed.

"Probably worse," Nana exhaled, slumping into the back of the chair.

Ben sat down next to Mason. "From what I observed, they have no intention of looking for another suspect. Nana's situation fits the narrative they want to build."

My stomach roiled with anger and fear. "You mean they can say they arrested the killer and get rid of the main leader of Honeysuckle all in one swoop?" I got off my knees and stomped in defiance where I stood. "They can't get away with that."

"Unfortunately, unless they actually do a true investigation to find the real killer, yes, they can." Ben wiped his hands down his face. "Or somebody else confesses to them directly."

I contemplated that option in my head. Nana cradled my chin in her hand. "Don't even think about it, Birdy. Besides, you were nowhere near her before she collapsed and there are too many people who can back that up."

Mason frowned. "What exactly do they think they have on Vivi?"

Ben looked to my grandmother for permission to speak. With a nod from her, he spoke. "It was witnessed by many that Priscilla went upstairs followed by her daughter. Ms. Vivi went upstairs a few minutes later and was still in the near vicinity when whatever happened took place. No one can verify her immediate whereabouts, so it's only her word that she was in the restroom collecting herself and not committing the murder."

"There has to be cameras posted all over. Didn't they check the tapes?" I asked.

Ben grimaced. "I asked them the same question. According to the chief, the cameras in the whole hotel have been offline for a month or so."

Mason scoffed. "That sounds about as true as a two-dollar bill, although it may prove advantageous to us now that they can't monitor our every move if they really aren't working."

"So, you have no idea what actually happened?" I turned

my attention to my grandmother, cursing the fact that she went up those blasted stairs in the first place.

Nana leaned forward and placed her forehead in her hands. "I know I shouldn't have confronted Priscilla. But after she wouldn't actually apologize to me and her treatment of her daughter, I thought somebody should finally stand up to that...that..."

"Witch with a capital *B*?" I finished.

My grandmother sighed. "I found Prissy and Peyton in the middle of a very heated argument. I couldn't decide whether or not to step in, but then I figured that unless I saw actual physical abuse, what they were discussing was really none of my business. I left them to hash things out and went to the restroom to gather my wits about me. When I came out, I followed all the commotion."

"And none of that provides you with an alibi," Mason stated, following the story to its natural conclusion. "This might be tougher than I thought."

"Yeah, but if they can't prove she wasn't around Priscilla in order to do something that would result in her death, then they also can't prove she did. The lack of evidence goes both ways." The world couldn't be this unfair, could it?

"There's a larger game involved—who died, who they can pin this on, and what that could do to the leadership structures of both places. It's possible someone is manipulating things to play out to their advantage, but that's going to take time to figure out." The detective stood and paced. "No, I still think our better play is to try and solve the murder quickly. Give them clear evidence that they can't manipulate."

Nana yawned, and I moved to rub her back. "You need to get some sleep."

"I'll go up to my room," she stated, pushing up from the arms of the chair with a groan.

"But the potential bugs," I countered.

She waved me off. "If they're listening in, all they'll hear is me snorin' up a storm."

I followed her to the door, and she stopped me. "I'm not feeble, Birdy. I can make it on my own. You need to stay here and work together with the detective." Nana hugged me tight and tilted her head so she could whisper in my ear. "I think this time you'll be the one who saves me."

The heavy responsibility enveloped me like a wet blanket, but I would shoulder whatever I needed to in order to prove her right. "I will," I muffled into her shoulder.

Ben waited for us to end the embrace. "I'll make sure you get to your room, Ms. Vivi. Then I'll go see Lily."

With the clank of the door, the quiet of the room surrounded Mason and me. I could duck under the quilted covers of his bed and lose myself to despair or I could pull up my big witch panties and dive right in.

Mason watched me with careful eyes until I challenged him. He shrugged. "I was trying my hardest to remember how we worked before. I'm aware that's how we first connected to each other. But when I search my memories, I can't find that thread anywhere."

Ironic he would mention a thread of connection. More than ever, I wished I had my magical talents back. As strong as I'd developed them, it might have been a real challenge to find what was used in Priscilla's murder, but at least I would have had a clear way to help.

Except, I wasn't the only witch with tracking abilities here in the hotel. "That's it," I exclaimed. "We need to find out what room my cousin is staying in."

"I don't think now's the time for you to get to know her. I'm sorry about that, by the way, but we really need to stay focused on finding something to clear your grandmother's name before it's too late," he repeated.

"That's not why I want to talk to her. If we're from the same family bloodline, then it stands to reason that she possesses some level of tracking powers like I do...used to." That last part stung, but I had to accept the truth so we could work with what we had.

Comprehension hit Mason and his face lit up. "I think I see where you're going with this. Should we go ask at the front desk?"

If the hotel was being compliant with the wardens, I suspected they wouldn't be very eager to help us run a covert investigation. "No, but I think I know somebody who might help us. Come on."

"You lead the way, Ms. Goodwin, and I'll follow," Mason stated from behind me.

I almost snorted and corrected him on how allowing me to take the point was *not* how we used to work together. But if we were moving forward, then we needed to forge new paths instead of trying to recreate the old ones.

Whoever my cousin really was deep down, she was about to find out exactly what being related to me truly meant. Whether she wanted to or not, she would be the instrument I used to clear my grandmother's name.

Chapter Eight

My plan to grab David and beg him to help us find Abigail's room number took us to the first-floor lobby. We walked around the front area and the empty conference rooms where signs from our canceled event still hung outside the doors. Instead of the hustle and bustle of hotel employees in uniforms hurrying to do their job, the place felt eerily empty. The two manning the front desk never looked in our direction or offered to help, throwing up an icy barrier of silence between us.

"Now what?" Mason asked, pressing the button for the elevators.

Since my initial plan failed, I didn't know if I wanted to be the one to come up with a second one. "We go to the floor I think she's on and knock on all the doors?"

I didn't miss the irony that if I still possessed my talents,

I might be able to find her on my own. Still, with every minute that ticked by, we lost time to do what had to be done.

The doors to the elevator slid open on a ding, and a few people shuffled out. Abigail walked out last. She gasped when I stepped in front of her and lurched to a quick stop.

"Oh, excuse me," she spat out and then looked up. "Hi, Charli."

Since I didn't know her well, I had a hard time deciphering the expression of confusion and hesitancy that bloomed across her face. I couldn't take the time to beat around the bush. Better to get straight to the point. "Abigail, can you take us to your room?"

"Why?" she gasped. Clearing her throat, she tried to recover. "I mean, you're welcome there, but it's a bit of a mess."

Mason stepped into the elevator and kept the doors from sliding closed. "Shall we?"

I liked that he pushed her to act rather than to stand around, hemming and hawing. Her body jerked a bit from warring with itself on whether or not to enter. I stepped up behind her, blocking any exit and encouraging her to take the few steps inside.

Once the doors closed, I maneuvered around her and stood next to Mason. "We wanted a chance to get to know you a little better, but my room's full of nosy girls and his room probably has a sleeping advocate in it. You're on the third floor, right?"

She nodded and took a deep breath. "I heard about your grandmother being held at the station all night. Is she okay?"

"Nana? She's tougher than an old boot. She'll be fine."

Mason touched the back of my hand with his, knowing my bravado covered up a whole lot of insecurity. The gesture let me know I wasn't completely alone in things, and I appreciated his support more than I could verbalize at the moment.

"I hope things work out for you," Abigail uttered in a shaky voice. "You'll have to excuse me. The past twenty-four hours have been filled with so much drama."

We reached her floor, and she exited, and I followed right behind her. "It's been a lot for all of us."

My new cousin didn't need to know how often Mason and I found ourselves around a dead body. I needed to convince her to work with us, not run away screaming.

With a beep from the scan of her room key, we entered her room. Nothing seemed out of place or in disarray. "Girl, if this is what you call messed up, then my house in Honeysuckle is downright dirty."

Abigail perked up when I talked about my life. "You own a house?"

"Inherited it when my great-uncle passed away. I live there with Beau, my vampire roommate," I explained.

Her eyes widened until the whites of them showed. "You have a vampire for a roommate? Isn't that really dangerous?"

I snort-giggled. "Beau, dangerous? Not in the least. He's big, cuddly, and can poof into a bat."

"No way." Abigail looked to the other side of the room, lost in thought. "I've always been told to avoid vampires."

Encouraged to keep her talking, I continued speaking about my hometown to loosen her up. "Then visiting me in Honeysuckle will knock your socks off. We not only have vampires, we've got a slew of fairies, gnomes, a leprechaun, a troll who loves Shakespeare...our town accepts pretty much any magical being who wants to live there."

"It sounds chaotic and wild," Abigail uttered. For a moment, I thought she might wilt away, but a wide smile that brightened her face surprised me.

"It can be unpredictable but also wonderful and welcoming." My real affection for Honeysuckle Hollow pushed away my worries for a brief moment until the fact my grandmother might not make it back there chilled me inside out.

"Where I'm staying right now, everybody keeps to themselves. There's not a whole lot of mixing amongst the magical community except at a meeting of all the big leaders once a month. At least that's what Ethan tells me." Resentment filled her last sentence.

"Who's Ethan?" I asked. "Your brother?"

Her nose wrinkled a bit. "No, he's a...he's part of the family."

The things I didn't know about my bloodline could fill an ocean. I didn't have time for pleasantries before I got down to business. "Listen, Abigail, since you're here trying to connect with me, then I'm going to extend the benefit of the doubt to you and get straight to the point. What kind of magical talents do you possess?"

"Oh, uh," she stammered, caught off guard. "I guess I have normal magic like any other witch."

"No, that's not what she means," corrected Mason.

I touched his arm to let me do the talking. "Listen, I've always had talents different from everyone else. They've been called bird-doggin' skills, hunting, or tracking. Whatever you call them, it means I could find things when I used them. Since I've found very few throughout the country with the same magic, I assume it has to be hereditary. What I'm asking is, can you track things down?"

Abigail looked down at the floor and back up at me. "Yes, our family has those abilities. Some are stronger than others. My powers are not as well developed."

I grabbed her hands, unable to contain my desperation. "As long as you've got some, that'll have to do. We need your help to prove my grandmother's innocence."

She frowned at me. "I don't understand. If you've got your own powers, then why do you need mine? I'm sure you're better at it than I am."

In life, we earned trust over time. Just because Abigail and I shared some DNA didn't afford her all of my secrets. "I think the more help we can get, the chances of clearing Nana's name will be better. Now, what are the limits to your talents? For me, it used to be I had to touch someone in order to find what they were looking for. Then I got strong enough

I didn't need them to do more than think about it. What about you?"

Her fingers twitched in my hands. "Holding something from the person associated with what I'm supposed to find makes things go much faster. But I can be given an assignment and find something based on the description from the person who desires it."

I raised my eyebrows. "And you think you're not strong? That's incredible. If we were to ask you to find the murder weapon, you could use your magic to locate it?" Hope rose in my chest.

"I don't think so." Her short reply poured cold water all over my expectations.

I let go of her. "But you said you could find things that were desired."

"If I have a full description because they know exactly what they want down to the finest detail," Abigail clarified. "What you're asking me to do is to search for something intangible unless you know what killed her, like a knife or a gun or something. Even then, the person who would be most connected to it is, well, dead."

Mason stepped forward. "If it could be arranged and you could be around the body, say, close enough to touch it, would you be able to determine what killed her? Or who did?"

Abigail scrunched up her face. "Who would want to touch a dead body?"

"Answer the question, please," I pressed, clinging on to the last of my patience.

My insistence annoyed her. "No, for most hunters, we work off of the connection to live people. There was a story that was told about an ancestor of ours who had the ability to find things connected to a dead body, but by using his powers, it drained him of his life."

"So, it's possible but comes at a cost?" I winced at the callousness of my question. "Sorry, I'm not suggesting you sacrifice your life."

Abigail picked at a scab on the side of her arm. "I don't think it's a true story anyway. It was something passed down more to warn us to be cautious with our powers than anything. My guess is whoever the ancestor was, he was lying and got killed for trying to grave rob or something."

I backed up and collapsed onto the edge of her bed. "So, that's it. We won't be able to figure out what caused Priscilla's death and Nana's innocence can't be proven."

"Well," started Abigail. "I would think her daughter would want to figure out who the killer is. She would possess the most desire to find out the truth. Maybe if you can get her to talk to you, you could use your own tracking magic to find the object."

My stomach sank. I glanced up at Mason, wondering if I should let this young woman I barely knew in on the truth of my life or not. But holding back information could only stand in our way or even become an unintended obstacle to our goal. He raised his eyebrows and tilted his head, allowing me to make my choice in what to reveal.

I took a deep breath and made my decision. "We have a

problem if we're going to count on me. The quick and dirty of it all is that I don't have my powers."

"What?" Abigail exclaimed.

I winced. "It's a much longer story, but the basics are that I had them, then through a spell, I lost them temporarily. When I was starting to get them back, another spell forced what I had into another witch." I couldn't say the next part without crying if I looked at Mason. "It was for a very good reason, and I would do it again."

The detective's breath quickened, and he stared at me with a mixture of awe and disbelief.

"I would do it again," I whispered, making sure he saw and heard my sincerity.

"Charli. I..." He cleared his throat, remembering that another person stood in the same room with us. "I think your suggestion is a good one, Abigail. I'll see what I can do to get Peyton to return to the hotel since we can't leave." Without hesitation, he bolted out the door.

"I feel like I'm missing something," my cousin said. "Are you two together?"

Some things about my life she hadn't earned the right to know yet. "No, he's just a good friend. I'm sorry to have bothered you. Nothing has gone like I'd planned, and I don't have the time to properly sit down and get to know you like we wanted." I reached out to touch her, and she flinched away. Whatever or whoever put that in her, I'd like to take them on. "I'm sorry, Abs."

My cousin gasped. "What did you call me?"

I realized my mistake and cringed. "Oops, I tend to do that. I call my friend Blythe, B. And Alison Kate is Ali Kat. I guess Abs just rolled off my tongue out of pure instinct. I won't use it again if it offends you."

Her eyes returned to the floor and her lips trembled. "Nobody calls me anything but Abigail. I was lying when I signed your note Abby. I wanted to sound friendly."

"Would you like me to call you Abby? I can do that," I offered.

She grinned and flushed a shade of pink that made her look healthier and more robust. "Okay, I'd like that. Or even Abs. It would be something that would be just between us."

"Because we're friends." I finished what I figured her thought was.

"Friends. I like that." She stuck out her hand and giggled. "Hi, my name is Abby."

I gripped her skin. "Hey, Abs. I'm Charli." We held onto each other for a long moment before I squeezed her once and let her go.

Feeling a bit more at ease, she piped up, "You know, it might not be all bad if you don't have your powers anymore. On the bright side, nobody will bug you or demand that you use them."

A piece of my heart hurt for her. "That sounds ominous. In Honeysuckle, I actually have my own business called Lost & Found where people can hire me to find things."

"You have a business? And people pay you?" Her draw dropped.

So many things we didn't know about each other, so little time. "Listen, Abs, when this whole thing is over, let's make a plan to really take the time to learn about each other. Deal?"

"Deal."

I smiled and turned to exit her room. She called after me. "Charli, wait." When I turned, I barely recognized the look of determination plastered on her face. "If you get more information and there's something concrete or a specific object that needs to be found, come get me and I'll locate it for you. Promise."

She had no idea how much her pledge meant to me. Needing to leave before more tears spilled, I nodded. "Thanks."

When the door closed leaving me on the other side in the hallway, I sank down to the floor, curled my knees up, and hugged them. Sadness and despair threatened to drag me down, but Abigail offered me a lifeline of hope at the last second with her promise. Instead of tears, tiny giggles gushed out of me, and I covered my mouth with both hands to contain them until I lost my breath.

With no tracking powers of my own, I had only my ideas and determination. Not so promising, but luckily, I had access to smarter people. Pushing myself off the floor, I found the staircase and ran up to the next floor in search of their help.

Chapter Nine

❧

"I've got sandwiches," Lily called out as she held the door to our room open with her foot. I rushed over to hold it so she could enter.

Her cousin Lavender followed behind. "And I brought drinks. No sweet tea to be found, but I did find a stash of soda cans in a closet."

Blythe helped bring in the armful of drinks. "Frosted fairy wings, you stole something, Lav?"

"Not stole, exactly. Let's call it liberated. They were trapped in a closet downstairs and needed help getting out to fulfill their purpose," Lavender joked. "Actually, I followed some of the staff and found them hoarding away supplies. Maybe they're stuck in here like we are?"

Lily passed around the food, and we took whatever sandwich she gave us. "I heard some of the other guests saying that the hotel isn't happy about the lockdown and won't be catering to us for much longer to encourage the wardens to wrap things up sooner."

"Well, they can't starve us," I managed while munching on my bite. "But they could give us cheese and crackers and call it food. It sounds like our deadline to solve things may be faster than we'd hoped if the hotel becomes uncooperative."

Mason wiped the corner of his mouth with a napkin. "Then let's share everything we've been able to figure out so far. In terms of the wardens, I think Chief Huxley has no intention to do more investigating. I ran into a couple of deputies talking to a few people, but they haven't assigned a detective to the case at all. If he could get away with it, I think the chief would arrest Ms. Vivi immediately, but thanks to Ben being an amazing advocate, he's having to deal with the legalities of cutting corners."

Lily sighed. "My boyfriend really is the best. He said he'd report back the second he returned. If we could access our spell phones, he could text me sooner."

Lee stopped inhaling his sandwich. "I know, I'm sorry things aren't going faster, but part of what makes the phones work is utilizing the magic from the area. There's something off about powers here that I can't quite figure out."

"You'll get there, sweetums." Alison Kate rubbed her husband's back. "I went down to the kitchens because when I get stressed, all I want to do is bake. I offered them my services, but they turned me down. I overheard a lot of what Lavender already said. The hotel management is considering ways to cut off as much comfort to those of us locked inside in order to end things quicker."

Lavender raised her hand, and I teased her for acting like we were in school. "There's a lot of gossip going around. One person said they saw your grandmother stab Priscilla from behind and another thought that there must have been poison in her drink."

"Which my grandmother had to have put in there, right?" I complained.

"People like to act like they know something or to share any tidbit that's dripping with juice," admitted Lavender.

Lily butted in, "Oh, and I heard other guests complaining to the front desk and suggesting that they be let out and to just keep the Honeysuckle group on lockdown. The longer this goes on, the more support there is for blaming your grandmother, Charli. If the guests get too frustrated, we could end up with an angry mob."

My stomach churned and I put down the rest of my sandwich. "I talked with Abigail. I wanted to see if she had the same tracking talents I did."

Blythe perked up. "That sounds promising. Did she say she could help?"

I swallowed down the lump in my throat and took an extra beat to ignore my rising panic. "Not really. Because we don't have access to the body or the medical examiner's findings or anything, we don't have an idea what there is to be tracked. She can't search for an abstract concept."

My best friend sat down next to me, the bed bouncing

with her presence. "I'm sorry it can't be you and your magic. I know that must hurt."

Others in the room uttered their apologies, too, and I realized I'd never allowed them to help me mourn the loss. I couldn't manage to vocalize my thanks for their support without losing my thin emotional control.

Mason cleared his throat, unable to look at me. "If we discovered concrete evidence for your cousin to use in her search, would she be able to do anything?"

I sniffed once to steady myself. "Yes, she promised if we had something tangible to find that she would help." Frustration with the entire situation overtook my fears and I pushed off the bed with a yell. "It's like we're trying to operate without the full picture. And we're too focused on my grandmother to see anything anyway. What are we missing?"

"A list of viable suspects," replied Mason.

"I can't believe they dismissed all the locals and let them go home," Blythe said. "Doesn't that imply that they aren't being considered suspects at all?"

"As a fellow warden, I'd like to have faith that they would continue to consider all possibilities until they have concrete evidence." The detective didn't have to finish for us to comprehend his unspoken doubt.

From somewhere in the city, bells chimed the midday hour. I gazed down at the busy sidewalk below and wondered if any of the passersby might be witches. "How strong are the wards on the hotel? Could they be breached at all?"

"I already tested them," Mason admitted. "Using my own

warden authority, I attempted at several different exits to break through their hold. Lee isn't wrong, there's something odd about the shared magic in the area. It's like it runs on a different frequency than ours."

"Frequency!" shouted Lee, bouncing to his feet. "I didn't think about it that way. The magic required is not operating on the same wavelength as ours. If I could figure out how to sync our spell phones to their magical frequencies, then I might be able to get things to work." He ran out the door, muttering to himself like a madman.

Ben entered the room, glancing behind him. "What's up with Lee?"

"I think my husband finally figured out how to get our spell phones to work." Alison Kate beamed with pride. "How did things go with the district advocates?"

Ben accepted a sandwich from Lily and sat down but didn't eat. "It's not looking good. We went back and forth over the current laws that dictate the wardens must do their due diligence and perform a full investigation. Trying to prove the local wardens aren't doing their job is a problem if both the ones who enforce the law and the ones who prosecute them are in collusion."

Sitting around with my friends discussing cases used to be thrilling and sometimes even fun. My little gang could combine their different points of view to guide me through the fog of confusion to find the clear path to solving the problem. Except this time, the problem was too close to my heart for me to see clearly.

"I'm sorry, Charli, I promise I won't let them get out of hand." Ben attempted a reassuring smile. "Even if they try to invoke *a priori assumption*, there are ways to delay it."

Unable to process more bad news, I couldn't hold back my annoyance. "Speak English, Ben," my voice wavered.

"It means they could make an arrest based solely on what they believe rather than by solid proof," interjected Mason. "I've dealt with a few who valued the 'old ways' over the law up North."

Overwhelmed, I lost the battle of trying to keep it all together. Gasping to find air, I weaved my way around the beds and friends and closed myself in the bathroom. Turning on the shower and the faucet of the sink to full blast, I shut the lid on the toilet and crumpled on top of it. My desperation surrounded me, and I surrendered to it, allowing the tears to flow without fighting them.

Hot steam billowed out from behind the shower curtain, and the curls in my hair grew fuzzy from the moisture. A fine sheen of sweat covered the surface of my skin until it mingled with my salty tears.

The door opened with a creak and I turned my back on whoever had volunteered to check on me. Heavy sobs racked my body, and I wept until nothing came out of me except a woeful keening. A kind touch petted my head and pulled my hair off my neck.

My grandmother crooned a song I hadn't heard from her in ages while her wrinkled hands worked their magic in calming me.

"Way up high in the old oak tree
A tiny little bird comes and sings to me
It chirps a song with joyful glee
And tries to tempt me with its plea

'The sun is high and the wind is free
So, come and fly away with me.'
All day long, it sings to me
'Come and fly away with me.'

'Oh, little bird, why can't you see?
I don't have wings so I can flee
I cannot come away with thee
And leave my life underneath the tree.'

BY THE THIRD VERSE, my sobs had abated, and I joined her in
the final verse like I used to do when I was little.

'Then I will bring the sky to thee
And sing to you where 'ere you be
For I see you and you see me
Way up high in the old oak tree'

Nana hugged me around my shoulders, restoring my faith and pushing away the edges of doubt in the best way she knew how. She repeated the song again, rocking me back and forth with her body behind me and her arms sheltering me.

"There, that's a little better," she teased after she finished, kissing the top of my head. "Do you think you could turn off the shower so I could see you through the mist?"

I chuckled despite myself and leaned forward, pushing the curtain out of the way and turning off the hot spray of water. "I made a mess in here, didn't I?"

"Messes can get cleaned up. Some days it takes more effort than others. This time around, it's going to require more than just you to get the job done, so stop trying to do it all yourself." She tossed a white fluffy towel at me so I could mop up the pooled water on the floor.

"Nana, I think even with all of us helping, we might not be able to clean up what they're trying to do to you." The truth tasted like Carolina clay, but we couldn't avoid it.

My grandmother leaned against the edge of the sink. The leather cord of her mojo bag she still wore stuck out of the top of her shirt. "Birdy, this may be an odd place to remind you of something important that's been passed down in our family for generations, but if I have to say these words in a bathroom, so be it. We Goodwins don't give up. If we find ourselves in a corner, we blast the wall behind us and make another way out."

"But without my powers, I can't help find anything," I protested. "Ben is having issues and fears the Charleston wardens are going to somehow skirt the law, and there's no way to prove your innocence."

Nana pushed off the sink and placed a hand on her hip. "Now you're willfully building walls to prevent from getting out of that corner you're in. Stop thinking about me, Bird. Look at the bigger picture and find another way out." She opened the door and exited the small bathroom.

Cooler air rushed in and cleared out the haze of steam. Standing in front of the mirror, I wrote Nana's name, Priscilla's, and the word *Murder* with my finger in the condensation on the mirror.

I wiped through my grandmother's name with a squeak, crossing it out. If we took her out of the focus, then we were left with the murder victim herself. My finger traced a circle around Priscilla's name, and droplets of water ran down the slick surface.

We needed to find who the grand dame of the local witches was. We were exposed to the surface of how things ran, but what were the gritty, dirty machinations behind the scenes?

I burst out of the bathroom to find my friends speaking in low voices. All eyes turned to me, and I pointed at Lavender. "People like to share juicy information. Spread it around until no one is sure what the truth really is."

Mason regarded me with thoughtfulness, his left eyebrow cocking up in comprehension. "You've come up with an idea."

"Well, clue the rest of us in," demanded Blythe.

"Gossip," I exclaimed. "If we want to figure out who might

be likely suspects other than Nana, we need to know the context of their lives here. Maybe she was sleeping with someone's husband and the jilted wife wanted to take her revenge. Or maybe she treated the other witches poorly and someone wanted to take her out for it or someone else can rise to social power with her out of the way. There are endless possibilities if we can find out the gossip."

Lily spoke up, "But if none of the Charleston witches are here, who's going to be our source?"

"Who sees everything but isn't seen?" I asked. When nobody could come up with the answer, I smiled for the first time in a while. "Those that don't matter. Those that are ignored because they're seen as being less than everyone else."

Nana nodded in approval. "Remember how Priscilla challenged me on the panel? One of Charleston's issues with Honeysuckle stemmed from our acceptance of all magical beings. Here, there's a huge group of beings who aren't treated equally. Like the fae."

"And I know at least one half-dryad who works right here in the hotel." I beamed at my burgeoning idea to gather information. "Let's spread out and see if we can track down any of the staff you might suspect could be fae and try to get them to talk to us. Our experiences in Honeysuckle and living a different kind of life could be the key to breaking the case wide open."

Renewed with a purpose, my friends filed out of the room. Ben stayed behind to speak with my grandmother and Mason waited for me outside the door.

"I'm glad our talk on the toilet did you good, Birdy. I'm proud of you," Nana crowed.

Her words bolstered my confidence in my task. "For what?"

"For blowing out the wall behind you. Now, go see what's on the other side."

Chapter Ten

Mason and I worked our way systematically up from the lobby to the top floor in search of David. We checked every corner and supply closet someone could use to hide.

"Maybe the staff was instructed not to talk to anybody. It feels like a ghost town in here. All we've seen are guests." I walked to the end of the hall and back. "Nope. Unless he's hiding in one of the rooms, I think we've run out of places to search."

The detective scratched the stubble on his face. "We can split up. I can't believe there isn't any staff at all."

I eyed the stairwell next to the elevators. "There's another floor."

"No, this is the top one," Mason disagreed.

Pulling open the metal door, I spotted another flight going

up. A chain hung across the stairs with a small sign dangling in the middle. *Employees Only*.

Mason joined me, and the heavy metal door clanged shut behind us. His observation about a clear way up the stairs nearly discouraged me. "But the wards should prevent us from going up there."

"Only one way to find out." With a determined grunt, I lifted my leg to step over the chain with the sign.

The detective yanked me back. "Don't ever breach a ward like that. You could get hurt or, if they've done their job properly, you could alert the local wardens to your attempts. Let me try."

He held up his hands in front of the stairs and concentrated. His eyebrows lifted high in astonishment. "Huh. The ward is still there, but it's not at full strength. There's a hole in it. Come on." With caution, he climbed over the chain and up the first two steps. "Stay in the middle like I did, and you should be fine."

I approached the stairs and twisted my body to step over the chain like I was trying to beat some invisible obstacle course in order to make sure I stayed in the middle.

Mason snickered at my attempts. "If I could make it through just fine, what makes you think you had to try and shrink yourself to fit? Let's see where this leads."

I let the detective lead the way in case he encountered another layer to the wards. We approached another steel door with no window. How were we to know what stood on the other side? Mason put his finger to his lips to keep me quiet, and with slow deliberation, he turned the knob and opened the door with care. A warm breeze replaced the stale air of the hotel and a beam of sun blinded me.

"I think we've stumbled on a crack in the wards." Mason triple-checked before he moved forward. "If there's nothing harmful on the other side, we might have found an important asset to help us with our investigation."

"Well, we won't know what's on the other side if you don't move," I teased. "Or you could let me go first and protect you instead. I'm pretty tough."

"I believe you."

I searched his face for the lie, but only the truth of his statement rested in his eyes. "Thank you. That means a lot." I shoved him aside and pushed my way into the sun before he could say anything else.

"Hey," he called after me.

The brightness from real sunlight disoriented me, and I shielded my eyes. Staying inside for so long made me appreciate the light that much more.

"I think I found where your dryad might be hiding," Mason said, walking past me and further onto the roof of the hotel.

Stark industrial vents gave way to green grass underneath our feet. Wildflowers sprouted in clumps all over. A hedge of roses in bright colors stopped our progress, but the sight beyond them both confused and delighted me. A small lake of crystal blue water with green reeds bending in the breeze on its shore sparkled in the afternoon sun.

"Glamour," Mason and I said at the same time.

A voice beyond the rose bushes whispered, "See, I told you it wouldn't work."

"Shh, stop talking," scolded someone in a high pitch. "They'll hear us."

A disembodied voice groaned, "Too late. Might as well knock it off."

With a few shimmers and the scent of a spring breeze, the view in front of us changed. Instead of an idyllic lakeside view, we found David sitting with a few other non-human looking friends on rickety rusted lawn chairs around a plastic kiddie pool behind short rose bushes. The half-dryad's green hair hung about his face. He pushed it back and greeted me.

"We've been looking everywhere for you. There are a few things I'd like you to explain to us." I waved at the others I didn't know yet.

One of them leaned forward. She blew out a big bubblegum bubble the same hue of pink as her hair and popped it. "I wouldn't trust them."

Something with wings circled my head, and I suppressed my instinct to wave it away. Two pixies flew around, chatting to David in their unintelligible voices.

"Yes, I know they're witches, Flit and Fleet. But they're from that town I was telling you about. Honeybee or something," explained David.

"Honeysuckle," I corrected.

"Right. The town where anybody is allowed to live freely," the half-dryad finished.

The pink-haired friend scoffed. "I highly doubt that."

"No, it's true. Witch, vampire, fairies, gnomes...we have all manner of people living in our small hometown." Mason's deep voice seemed out of place with the company we kept.

The chair beneath her creaked as she pushed herself out of it, landing on her feet and pointing at her back. "Even me? This is what happens when a fairy falls in love with a witch." Two wings fluttered, but their tiny iridescent size wouldn't lift her off the ground because they didn't come close to matching the proportions of her body.

"Rayna," David pleaded.

The diminutive young woman popped her gum again. "My biological father ran off, unwilling to legitimize my half-breed status. And when I grew too big to fit in with my mother's clan, she kicked me out. I've got no place to go and nothing I'm good for except doing the laundry in the bowels of this place. If you think I'll give that up to talk to you two, then you're exactly as smart as I think all witches are." She stomped off, ignoring her friends' pleas.

David pushed his green hair out of his face. "I'm sorry about Rayna. It's taken her a long time to settle down somewhere. And if you're going to ask me about the things I think you might, then I can understand. In fact, if no one else is willing to speak plain and true, then you need to leave now."

The two pixies dipped in the air, their voices buzzing in harsh tones. One of them tugged the other's arm. The one who didn't want to move yanked itself free and flew to hide behind David, crawling out from underneath the green strands of his hair.

"Fleet, why don't you stay and listen? If things get too scary, you can leave," the half-dryad suggested. He grinned when the other pixie ventured out from its hiding place to rejoin its friend.

"I don't want to make anyone uncomfortable, but if you would give us a chance, I think you would see we mean you no harm." Mason held up his hands as if in surrender.

"David, this is about my grandmother. If you could help us, you might be able to save her," I pleaded. "Please."

He moved aside and offered me the seat he'd vacated. I thanked him and sat down. Mason refused Rayna's empty chair, choosing to stand next to me.

"The floor, or more correctly, the roof is yours." David sat down in the half-fairy's chair ready to listen.

I explained the situation so they could all understand the stakes at hand and maybe forgive my determination to push to learn as much as possible as soon as possible. Once I felt like I'd won a bit of their trust, I gripped the metal arms of the chair to steady myself.

"We need to know more about Priscilla Ravenel Legare," I explained. "More importantly, we need to know who might have wanted to punch her ticket."

A slightly plain and short figure stepped out from behind a bush we hadn't noticed. "I think the easier answer would be who *didn't* want her dead. It'd be a much shorter list."

"But if we're trying to be helpful, Molly, perhaps you could give them some insight to what life is like in their household since your sister still works for them." David stood up to offer her his seat.

Molly shook her head no and stayed where she was. "I won't say anything that might get Meg in trouble. She's protective of her job, and I won't betray her. We brownies are fiercely loyal." Just when I doubted we'd be able to learn anything useful, she held up her finger. "I mean it when I say the list of people who might have done it will be long. But I'll try to help you narrow it down."

She listed off all the top witches who might be a contender to take over as proverbial leader in the witch community. "See, Priscilla didn't hold an official title. She wasn't on the witch council. Hers was more an enforced position through her bullying and cunning skills at using information to get what she wanted."

"She blackmailed people?" Mason asked.

"Oh, her hands were clean. Always. But if you traced all the lines of manipulation going on under the surface, almost all of them would lead back to her." The look of disgust on the brownie's face matched the curdling in my stomach.

David scoffed. "You don't know the half of what she and her kind have done. Do you know why I'm here? It's not because I think I can't belong anywhere. It's because two generations ago, my great-grandfather took my great-grandmother to a healer here in town. Because he wasn't a witch, he was given a simple tonic that did absolutely nothing for her. But that didn't stop the healer from charging him an amount of money my great-grandfather couldn't pay."

Although it was off topic, I needed to know how the story of his descendent wove in and around the half-dryad's tale. "What happened?"

David hid his face with his hair again. "After my great-grandmother didn't get better, my great-grandfather wanted to raise enough money to take her to a different healer in a town not too far from here that would help any magical beings. A witch in town offered to pay for the treatment if my kin would work for him."

"It's the old company system," Mason interjected. "My guess is that your great-grandfather accrued even more debt despite performing the duties of his job. And that debt rolled into bigger debt."

"Until I am the last in our line to try and take our family name off the ledger once and for all. Except I cannot rise above a certain position within the workforce. Another rule enforced by Priscilla." David crossed his arms and sat back in his chair.

His story spoke of a horrible practice not only allowed but also pushed into action by the elite witches of Charleston. As much as I sympathized with him, the confession suggested something more sinister.

"You do realize you have given a reason for all of the non-witches who are in the same boat as you to hate Priscilla. That means there could be countless perpetrators." The detective paused, waiting for them to catch on. "That includes you."

David and Molly gazed at each other with great surprise until giggles burst out of them. The two pixies tittered while they hovered.

"How does the possibility that you're a suspect not scare you?" I asked.

David attempted to stop laughing. "Because there's no way anyone like us could harm her. We physically can't. It's part of the enchantment over the city. It dampens any magic we possess until we're almost shells of who we should be. And it makes it impossible if we wanted to retaliate."

"Some have made it out. Most of us who end up here get caught in a cycle we can't break free from. For me, I won't leave my sister and she won't leave the family. Probably now more than ever." Molly spat on the ground.

"I don't understand. If Priscilla was so bad, then why does your sister stay?" Mason asked.

Molly's prominent brow furrowed underneath her wiry bangs. "I can't say, I already told you. But if you get a chance, you should try talking directly to the daughter. Now that her mother's gone...no, I won't say any more about them." The brownie turned to leave. "I wish you luck in the impossible task before you. In this town, if you're not one of them, then there's really no help for you."

I wanted to grab her and force her to tell me more. A few names of witches who might try to take Priscilla's place of power wouldn't guarantee the wardens would investigate them. And with her refusal to give specific information about the family, we'd hit another dead end.

"We're never going to solve this," I muttered under my breath.

The two pixies rose higher in the air from where they hovered and bounced in tandem. One of them flitted to David and spoke in his ear.

"Flit's asking me why you haven't asked either him or his sister any questions," the half-dryad conveyed to us.

"My deepest apologies, Flit," I addressed the one bobbing next to David. "Is there anything you can tell us about Priscilla?"

The pixie's wings wavered in quick pulses. The high-pitched buzz of his voice grew louder in his excitement.

"He says that nobody ever takes notice of their kind and that he and Fleet saw your grandmother. Hold on one moment." David held up his finger to allow the pixie to tell him more. "Fleet saw your grandmother enter the bathroom while the mean lady and her offspring argued."

"Excuse me, Fleet and Flit," Mason spoke in a gentler tone. "But would you be willing to testify to that fact?"

The pixies didn't have to speak to David. The half-dryad challenged the detective. "Would it matter if they did? No one's going to accept the word of a pixie. And if they revealed what they saw, their own lives could be in jeopardy. But they wanted you to know so you wouldn't worry about whether or not your grandmother killed Priscilla. They're positive she didn't."

I'd never doubted Nana's innocence, but I appreciated the gesture. "Thank you for that." I gave a slight bow of my head to both pixies.

Fleet rushed over to David and pushed her brother out of the way, speaking in such a high tone I could barely hear her at all. Whatever she conveyed was long, and my knee bounced with anticipation.

David spoke for the pixie. "She says Molly's right about the offspring, er, I guess Ms. Peyton. She was arguing a lot with her mother, more than just that night. Also, she wants to know if she and her brother were willing to try to help by talking to the wardens, would you allow them to come back to your town with you so they could stay safe?"

I almost choked up at the enormity of the offer made by two of the smallest fae. "Of course, you can. Our town was founded as a safe haven for all magical beings who wanted to live in peace with each other."

David's eyes brightened. "Does that offer stand for anyone?"

Mason spoke up before me. "If you want to come live in Honeysuckle, you can stay with me until you find a place to call home."

The detective's kindness even during a time of crisis bowled me over. I don't know why I should be surprised. He always had a kind heart. But for some reason, I felt like I was getting to know how much goodness lived inside of him for the first time.

David jumped out of his seat, toppling the rickety thing

over. "Then I need to find you more staff who will talk to you."

I stopped him from running off. "You know, you don't have to do anything to live in Honeysuckle other than want to be there. There's no debt or anything that has to be paid."

The half-dryad's breath caught. His voice quivered as he spoke. "And for that, I will work hard to find you others who might be able to give you what you need. Not because I have to, but because, for the first time, it's a pleasure to work for a witch."

"You're not working for us. You're working *with* us," corrected Mason.

David's smile spread across his face from ear to ear. "Even better. Maybe the more you have working *with* you, the better chance you might have in fighting."

I followed behind the half-dryad and the pixies. When they made it inside the stairwell, I stopped. "Hey, why does the ward not work on the roof?"

David turned around to look up. "Because that's our only space of refuge. All of us fae in the hotel sacrificed a bit of our powers to protect that area. I guess the wardens' magic couldn't penetrate it or something."

Mason held me back before entering the top floor of the hotel. "I think the fae may still hold more magic than they think. It's something to consider if we need help in a tight spot."

I shook my head. "The witches' treatment of them is so awful, I'd like to resurrect Priscilla and kill her again."

Mason pressed his hand over my mouth. "Don't say things like that out in the open. You have no idea who might be listening or how they might use that against you."

For a brief moment, a familiar heat rose in my body. Wondering if he felt anything at all, I risked looking up at him. His eyes stared into mine as if I were a puzzle he needed to solve.

"Are you two coming?" David hissed in a low voice.

Unable to wait, I licked his palm, and he withdrew his hand with a mock expression of disgust. With the brief moment between us well and truly over, I skipped down the last steps and followed the half-dryad.

For the first time since being stuck here, I allowed hope to come out of the dark hiding place I'd forced it into. My heart beat fast, knowing that my new alliance might be the key to get us out of everything, including a locked down hotel.

Chapter Eleven

I grabbed Ben's face with both my hands. "I could kiss you, you crazy advocate! You are the absolute best, especially when you're being the worst!"

"Uh, thanks?" my friend uttered through his mouth all squished from my enthusiastic hold.

"Hands off my man, girlie," warned Lily.

I let go of Ben and stuck out my tongue at her. "Aw, come on. Just a little one?" I teased, pinching two fingers together. "He deserves a medal or something."

Ben's cheeks blushed a bright pink, but the glint in his eyes conveyed his true pride. "Hey, it's not my fault if the chief of wardens here in Charleston doesn't protect his case files. If he leaves them sitting on the table in front of me so I can take pictures of the contents, then he's giving me permission *in absentia*."

"I thought our spell phones weren't working," I commented, taking the seat at the desk and trying not to get too nosy about some of Mason's things laid out on it. A part of me wanted to rummage around the detective and Ben's room to see if I could learn something new about him, but my excitement over what Ben had to share overrode my curiosity.

"In the hotel, they won't work," corrected Ben. "I think they forgot to check me for my phone before bringing me into the station. I may have been playing up the dumb yokel witch advocate role a bit much so they didn't take me seriously."

"Did you manage to get any calls out?" Mason asked.

The sides of Ben's mouth dropped. "I didn't have much time on my own, and I didn't want them to confiscate the phone. When I did have a few seconds by myself, I used them to take the pictures. I'm hoping Lee will figure things out so we can make some calls soon."

We gathered around while our crafty friend pulled up his clandestine pictures of the case files. It took us a few moments of trying to climb over each other to see to realize we could only look one at a time.

"Mason first," I declared. "He knows the warden-ese language."

The detective chuckled, accepting the spell phone from Ben. "Warden-ese? I'm multi-lingual now?" He held the phone up for a closer look. "If I'm not mistaken, this isn't your actual phone, is it?"

"Lee's got mine. He wanted to experiment on an older

phone first rather than his newer one, so we swapped. I'm actually glad, because this one has a better camera. Can you enlarge it enough to read?" Ben pointed at the screen.

Mason manipulated the size of the first picture and dismissed it with a swipe. A few pages later, he took a closer concerned look. "The only notes they have at all are the ones taken the night of the murder. There has been no new questioning since then."

"No one from Charleston has been interviewed further?" I asked.

The detective read through more. "No, all of their findings so far are based off the observations from the first night. I'm included as interfering in an unofficial capacity. I guess interfering is what they call insuring everything was secure before they showed up."

"You know they're not going to give you any credit." I moved around Mason to look over his shoulder and reached over him to point at the screen. "Is there anything in there at all that could give us something to work with?"

He batted my hand away. "Give me a second."

It took the detective a few minutes of reading through all the documents Ben had managed to snap until something grabbed his attention. "This is interesting. I was scrolling too fast before to notice it. It's an incomplete form, but its contents probably weren't supposed to be included in the case file. Ben, I think you struck gold."

"Good. I'd hate to think I could be disbarred for something worthless." My advocate friend tried to play it off like he didn't care, but it would break him if he lost his ability to do the job he loved.

"Charli," Mason called out. "I think it's time to go back to your cousin. It says here that Peyton Legare called into the station and inquired whether or not a certain ring had been logged into evidence along with her mother's other possessions. There's a sticky note taped to it with a penciled message. Whichever warden looked into the inquiry found a gold wedding band and a large three-diamond gold ring. But there's a missing third ring unaccounted for."

"Finally!" I exclaimed. "Now, we've got something to search for. Are there any details about the ring? The more we have to go on, the more connection Abigail might be able to make to it while searching."

Mason checked the images again. "No. Just the notes about it not being with the other evidence they took from the body."

"It'll have to do." I got on my feet, ready to run out the door and rush upstairs to my cousin's room.

Ben grabbed my arm before I could pass him. "Hold on a second. You can't go trying to find the ring we found out about through a case file I illegally took pictures of and brought to you. What happens if you do locate it? How are you going to explain how you knew about it without involving my actions?"

My stomach dropped at the choice I had to make. Use the one sliver of information we'd gathered in order to move forward in our quest to save Nana at the expense of my friend's career? Or ignore the ring and let things play out?

"We could find it and not tell anyone," I bargained.

"As if you could." Lily put her arm around Ben's waist. "I know you, Charli. The second you figured out who had the ring, you'd be pushing for the wardens to arrest them and clear your grandmother. I don't blame you, but if you do that, Ben's entire career and everything he's worked for would be over. You can't do that to him."

"You can't expect me to do nothing." I pointed at her. "If this were your grandmother, you know you would do anything you could to help her. That's all I want to do."

Ben's stern expression relaxed. "You know, she's right. Maybe it's worth the risk. It's possible she could have heard about the ring from someone else. They probably couldn't prove where the information came from in the first place."

"Yeah, but even if she finds the person standing in the middle of the Hyperion Hall dancing around naked except for wearing the ring on his or her finger, Charli can't prove that person actually murdered Priscilla. So why take the risk?" Lily painted a vivid picture I wanted to scrub from my mind with a thousand bars of soap.

I wanted to argue, but she had a valid point. We all fell silent, contemplating how to handle the situation. I really didn't want to hurt Ben, but I was desperate to protect my grandmother. And I couldn't tell anybody in the room, but I wanted to see how Abigail's magic worked. Did she do things like I do...did? Were her abilities far more advanced than mine? Maybe I wanted to see her in action as a way to feel more of a connection. To feel more related.

Exasperated, I made my choice. "I'm tired of waiting around in our rooms and making plans. I want to be out there doing something, anything, to move things forward. And now I have a tangible object I can use. I'm sorry, Ben and Lily, but—"

A frantic knocking on the door interrupted me. Blythe pushed inside the room once Mason let her in. Lavender followed behind with a satisfied grin.

"That new friend of yours, David, is a truly remarkable guy. He helped us talk to a lot of the kitchen and cleaning staff of the hotel." Blythe spoke so fast, her voice came out breathy. "It turns out everything isn't quite so polished and perfect with the Charleston coven as a whole."

Lavender jumped in, "Priscilla wanted to present a unified front for the conference, but it seems that some witches didn't appreciate how she did things and wanted to make big changes not only to their group at large but also to the magical community of Charleston."

"So, Charleston isn't perfect? I'm shocked," I mocked.

Lowering her voice as if someone could hear us, Lavender continued. "You were right that some of the staff here go unseen but see and hear everything, Charli. At some event held at the Hyperion Hall two months ago, there was a huge fight that split people into factions of loyalties, not to mention the list of people who Priscilla practically ruined. I wrote all the names down that the people David helped us talk to could remember."

Ben held out his hand. "Let me see this list, please. I've been hearing so many names while dealing with the wardens and the district advocate, I might be able to identify some of them." He read through the names and handed it to Mason. "Out of the twenty or so names, I recognize a few. But there's one here that sticks out."

Mason frowned while he inspected the list until he got to the one Ben had noticed. "Wasn't she the one who was helping Priscilla run the panel in the morning?"

"Who was? Frances Something? She's on the list?" I asked, itching to take a look at the names.

"Unless there are two women named Frances, according to a very shy sprite who was on bathroom cleaning duty at the time, she heard Priscilla yell out that name specifically while fighting with another lady in one of the hotel bathrooms on the first floor," Lavender confirmed. "Because the sprite was frightened, she couldn't quite remember what the fight was about, but she said the scary lady said something about the price the other one had to pay to recover her reputation."

"When was this?" Mason asked.

Lavender shook her head. "I'm sorry, but I don't think the poor creature would know for sure. It took a lot of coaxing to get her to talk to me, and, I'm ashamed to say it, I may have invaded her head a little in order to understand what she was saying. This fight could have been last week or last year. Her fear of what might happen to her for divulging anything to us clouded her memories."

My friend's blossoming psychic abilities impressed me, although I knew her grandmother had been diligently teaching both cousins. They had been instrumental in helping as much as possible with Mason's recovery from having his memories stripped by a rogue psychic. I wished either one of them could read every person's mind to help us catch the killer, but I'd heard Lavender admit their newer abilities weren't as reliable and could take a lot out of them when used.

"That David is really trying to help us. Whatever you said to him, he's really motivated," remarked Blythe.

"He thinks he'd like to move to Honeysuckle," Mason said. "He seems to think he has to earn his way into our town."

"Poor guy, but he's trying really hard and getting results. I hope he doesn't get caught by the hotel management. He could lose his job," Blythe worried.

I didn't want the half-dryad to make too much noise or earn himself any unwanted attention. For all we knew, the wardens had people watching us, and he didn't have the protection of being a witch to keep him from getting in too much hot water.

"So, we've managed to narrow it down to a list of locals who might have reasons to hold a grudge against Priscilla. Unless we can talk to them directly, I don't know what else we can do with the knowledge," Lily pointed out. When the room grew quiet, she cringed. "Sorry to be the wet blanket."

"But you're right," I admitted. "We need to figure out how to talk to at least some Charleston folks." Tapping my finger against my lip, I recalled something I'd heard at the first panel. "I think I have an idea. I'm going to go find my cousin."

Lily plucked the hem of my shirt to hold me back. "I thought you understood the potential consequences for Ben if you go looking for the ring."

I patted her hand to reassure her. "Not Abigail. Clementine. Tucker said he knew Peyton back in college and that she was pretty nice. Maybe he could come up with a way to convince her to come to the hotel. It's a long shot, but hey, my whole life has been based on those."

"I'll come with you," volunteered Mason.

Everyone quieted down, their eyes bouncing between the detective and me. The tension around us grew thick while they judged his motives and my reaction.

In truth, I wanted him to come with me for no other reason than desiring to be around him in any capacity. Plus, he helped me see things in different ways. I had some of my best "eureka" moments around him. But if I seemed too eager to accept his company, my friends might think there was something going on between us other than building a friendship.

"If you want to. Whatever." Inside, I cringed, hoping my fake indifference would make the rest of them stop staring at us.

Ignoring the audience, Mason closed the distance between

us and placed his hand at the small of my back. "You've been doing pretty good at taking the lead so far. I'll follow you."

It took a considerable amount of effort to ignore the warm tingles spreading through my body and avoid my friend's gleeful faces while they watched me and the detective working together. I closed my eyes and prayed to the Fates something could happen to take the attention off of us.

The door flung open with a bang. "I did it! I got the spell phone to work," Lee declared.

"Did you have to almost spellcast the door off its hinges to tell us?" Blythe scolded. "Something like you breaking through the magical enforcement's wards with the spell phones might be information we don't want everyone knowing."

Lee ignored her and waved around what used to be Ben's phone. "Mason's idea was a great seed that planted itself in my brain. If we think about our magic working like electricity, there are different wavelengths—"

"We don't have time to understand how you did it. Can you get everybody's spell phone working?" I asked.

Our genius pushed his glasses up his nose. "Only those from Honeysuckle. Our spell phones run a little differently due to working with the special magic of our town. I need to do a few more rounds of testing and then I can push through the update. Keep your phones on you and you should receive a text when I finish."

"How long until our phones work?" pushed Mason.

"Well, I haven't gotten this one to work consistently. So, I need to try and perfect my spellcasting. And once I do, I can't send an update too fast to the rest of them because I could fry everyone's spell phone. So best guess, sometime tonight. Maybe tomorrow." Lee glanced around the room, suddenly aware of his surrounding environment. "What's going on? Y'all look like you were about to do something and I interrupted."

"We were and you did," I joked. "We're proud of you and glad you're on our side, not theirs." Patting his back, I leaned in so only he could hear me. "But considering our circumstances, try really hard to make it sometime tonight." I kissed him on the cheek and headed out into the hallway.

My friend's brilliant brain added one extra move on the chessboard to help us solve the murder and save Nana. If I could get Tucker's help, we might be able to change the game all together.

Chapter Twelve

Next time a large group from Honeysuckle went anywhere, we needed to keep an updated list of the rooms everyone was staying in. Without the use of our spell phones, Mason and I had no way of knowing which room Clementine and Tucker occupied. Deciding we had to be brave and ask the front desk staff, we made our way downstairs.

Only one young man in a rumpled suit sat behind the counter. At first, he ignored us, but as we got closer, his blank countenance changed to one of annoyance. "What do you want?"

I understood the frustration of the situation, but we still deserved a modicum of respect. My fingers itched to aim a stinging hex at him, but Nana always said an ounce of spite was worth a pound of unicorn manure.

Instead, I put on my best Southern belle act. "Well, bless your heart, you must be about as tired as we are being stuck in here. Has anyone even brought you something to eat or drink?" I asked, pouring a little extra sickeningly sweet syrup on my Southern drawl.

Thrown off by my concern for him, the employee relaxed. "No, but my break is coming up soon. I just hope there's still something left for me to eat. And what about you? Is there something you two need?"

Jackpot. Once again, Nana's wisdom saved the day. "I'm looking for my cousin and her husband, Mr. and Mrs. Tucker Hawthorne? I've completely forgotten what room they're staying in," I read his name tag, "Stuart."

Without complaint, he checked through the records. "It looks like they're in room 407. But that name sounds familiar. Is he some kind of official or something?"

Confused, I leaned on the counter. "Tucker serves on our town council."

Stuart nodded his head. "I think that's what the man said. He demanded to talk to our on-site manager and wouldn't leave the lobby until he was seen."

Mason chortled. "Sounds like him."

"What was Tucker doing talking to management?" I wondered out the side of my mouth to the detective.

The young man pointed to a hallway to his left. "I don't know what they worked out, but now people can go out into the courtyard that you can access down there."

"We can go outside?" In my excitement, I spoke a little too loud.

Although Mason and I had been on the roof, we didn't want to risk it again without knowing why the wards didn't work right up there. To have an outdoor space where we could take a break from being cooped up inside would be a major relief.

"Your cousin's husband must be very persuasive. Management contacted the wardens to modify the wards to include the courtyard not too long ago. I think you can find both of them out there," Stuart explained.

"Are the wardens still here?" Mason stood taller, sounding more professional.

"There's a group of them that came, and I haven't noticed them leave through the front doors yet." Stuart glanced around him and crooked his finger for us to come closer. "I heard them talking about going over to the Hyperion Hall to find something. One of them said what they were looking for might close the case and they could let everyone out of here."

Mason shifted his body to hide the fact he was touching my hand. Although we suspected we knew what the wardens were tasked to find, we didn't need an employee who was willing to spread information knowing how much information we'd been able to discover.

I pointed in the direction of the courtyard. "This way?"

"Yeah." Stuart managed a small grin before being interrupted by one of his colleagues joining him behind the desk. "Guess it's my break time. I hope you find your cousin."

I wanted to sprint to the courtyard and stand in the sun, but such behavior wouldn't be very becoming. Even though we must be beyond basic polite manners by now in our circumstances, I still couldn't do anything that might make Nana disappointed in me.

Mason opened the glass door, and we both stepped into daylight. A garden water feature gurgled in the middle of the space and beautiful planters full of blooming flowers softened the concrete and brick.

"Charli," Tucker called out. He and Clementine sat at a table on the far side, hidden behind a potted palm.

My cousin's husband stood up as we joined them and shook the detective's hand. "I'm hoping the two of you have been as busy as we've been trying to get a few things done. I know this isn't the best environment to talk, but at least we can breathe out here. It's getting a bit stifling inside."

"How did you manage to get them to change the wards?" I accepted a bottle of water from my cousin before Tucker returned to his seat, taking a few sips before offering it to Mason.

Clementine beamed at her husband. "He didn't give them a choice. The circumstances won't last forever, and in the end, Charleston will have to find a way to deal with us. Tucker reminded them that the relationship could be friendly or not."

Tucker sat up straighter bolstered by his wife's pride. "Since our last encounter with representatives from the city was bungled, I offered them a way to rectify the transgression."

My cousin's eyes dropped to the table at the mention of Priscilla's brother, Calhoun, and his attempt to overthrow Honeysuckle. Her mother, my Aunt Nora, had been a part of Calhoun's plans. It didn't escape my notice when Tucker reached out to squeeze Clementine's hand, and I smiled at his gesture of love and support.

"There's not much I'm willing to tell you while we're out here in the open. But we've managed to find out a few things with our own investigation," Mason informed.

Tucker weaved his fingers through his wife's and grinned. "I figured you two would be on the job. Anything I can do to help?"

"Yes." I checked the area for anybody hiding, especially any beings that were used to being ignored. I leaned forward and spoke low. "Can you manage to get Peyton here somehow? We need to have access to her in order to solidify our details. Actually, I wish we could call everyone back, but that's not likely."

My cousin and Tucker looked at each other and chuckled. Clementine blushed. "I may have helped you without knowing it. Per my suggestion, Tucker negotiated contacting Peyton already."

"I've already called her and suggested that, as a show of good faith that we were not being held here as inadvertent prisoners of the Charleston witches' community and to solve the issue of the hotel staff serving us the bare minimum, maybe she and a few others could arrange a potluck dinner for tonight." Tucker leaned back in his seat, his cockiness more than earned.

"That's actually brilliant," Mason admitted. "Depending on who else comes to deliver the food, we might even have access to some of the ones on the list."

"What list?" Clementine asked.

The door to the courtyard opened, and all four of us shut our mouths, standing up to see who had interrupted.

I pushed a few fronds of the palmetto out of the way. "Abigail!"

The poor girl jumped in surprise. "Oh, I didn't know anyone else was out here. I'm so glad we have a place we can go outside."

Tucker and Clementine stiffened when Abigail approached our table. She offered a weak smile to me but shuffled in shyness around the others.

"Let me introduce you. This is Tucker Hawthorne and his wife, Clementine. I think you met Mason last night." I gestured at each of them. "This is Abigail Wilson, and she came here specifically to meet with me."

Clementine stood up and shook her hand. "And how do you know Charli?"

"I'm her cousin." Abigail's voice wavered and she cleared her throat and tried again. "Our family found her after a long search, and Charli and I arranged to meet here for the first time."

"Cousin?" Clementine's eyebrows rose until they hid underneath her bangs.

"Yeah, uh, she left me a note at my house after the barbecue contest. I guess I hadn't told you yet?" I stammered, rubbing the back of my neck. I never expected to find myself in such an awkward position between my two families.

Clementine shook her head. "But I've been so busy helping Tucker out that we haven't had our usual coffee dates." She offered the newcomer her seat. "It's nice to meet you, Abigail."

"Oh, I don't want to bother all of you." My newly found cousin took a step away from the table. "I just came out here to get some fresh air when the person at the front desk told me this place wasn't off limits anymore."

If the staff was informing guests about the new open space, it wouldn't be long until it was overrun. "It's fine, I actually want to talk with you in private, Abs." I watched my cousin brighten from my use of a nickname.

"And I want to check and see if the wardens are still here. Maybe they'll treat me with professional courtesy and fill me in." Mason excused himself and left.

A few other people entered the courtyard, and the rest of us made our way back inside. I reassured Abigail that I would be right with her and pulled Clementine and Tucker to the side.

"Keep me up to date of when and where Peyton and other locals are going to show up at the hotel. They may be our last hope to discover anything that might help keep Nana out of trouble," I explained.

"If there's anything else you need, you let me know." Tucker's natural authority rolled off of him. He looked over my shoulder at Abigail. "I'm happy for you that you finally found someone from your biological family. I know that's always been something you've wanted." His expression softened, and I appreciated his genuine care for me.

"Can you trust her?" Clementine questioned. "I know I don't have much of a right since you and I haven't always been that close."

"I'm learning whether or not she can be trusted. This hasn't been the best environment to get to know each other, but in the long run, we may appreciate her being here." I touched my cousin's arm. "And our past doesn't define us. Who we are to each other right now does. As Nana always told me while I was growing up, blood doesn't make a family. Love does."

Clementine pondered the saying, a little sadness reaching her eyes. "I like that. I wish my mother had accepted that years ago or that I hadn't listened to her for so long."

"You're changing things now, darling." Tucker kissed the top of her head.

It wasn't that long ago when my ex-fiancé, my cousin, and I were like oil and water. After what happened with Tucker's father, my aunt, and a few times my life was threatened, time proved it really worked as a healer.

I hugged Clementine harder than usual and thanked

Tucker one more time for representing our small town so well. My cousin touched my arm as I turned to leave and pulled me in so she could whisper to me.

"Family looks out for each other, so I want you to be cautious. There's something about her that, I don't know, doesn't quite fit. She might just be a very nervous person, but...I don't know." Clementine sighed and kissed my cheek. "Just be careful."

"I will," I promised. When I turned to face Abigail, my heart tore a little bit between my family of love and the one bonded by blood. I'd have to find a way to bring them both together.

Abigail shrugged when I approached her. "I'm sorry for interrupting you."

"No, I was actually going to come find you. Remember that promise you made to me earlier?" I waited for her to catch on.

"Oh, yes." She nodded with enthusiasm.

I looped our arms together and pulled her with me. "I'm cashing it in. Let's go somewhere more private so I can fill you in."

Now that Tucker had managed to create a reason for Peyton to come to the hotel, I could engage Abigail in finding the ring and goad Priscilla's daughter into revealing the information herself. Ben wouldn't be at risk anymore, and maybe we could find the real killer before the end of the night.

Chapter Thirteen

Abigail and I stood in the middle of the Hyperion Hall after Mason snuck us in. The wardens who'd been in the larger events building forgot to raise the shield before they left.

"I think I'll leave you two to work on your own," he declared. "Good luck."

As he reached the door, I rushed over to him, a sudden sense of panic filling me. "You don't have to go."

Mason turned to face me. "You can do this, Charli. I know it might be hard to watch her do what you used to be able to, but maybe it'll be good for you to see."

"Or incredibly frustrating," I breathed out, appreciating how he guessed exactly what bothered me.

He took both my hands in his, shocking me out of my

doubt. "I don't think I've ever thanked you properly for your sacrifice."

"Mason, I—"

"No, just let me finish," he interrupted. It took him a few heavy moments to gather his courage. "I've been thinking about the past few months and how I've been focused solely on my own frustrations. It's taken me a while to try and see things from your perspective, and I honestly think you're the one who lost the most."

I squeezed his hands. "I'm fine. Really." If we continued down the path I thought he was going, I might turn into a useless puddle of emotions.

Mason refused to let me pull away from his grip. "You lost a relationship and your special magic all at the same time. I may not remember what you were like before, but I can see what a good heart you have. One thing I do know about you loud and clear is that you don't need me to be with you while you and your cousin do your thing. You're a strong woman, Charli."

I couldn't meet his gaze any longer. Looking away, I cursed the few tears that escaped, proving how weak I really was. I appreciated his attempts at forging a new connection with me, but I wasn't done mourning what we had lost just yet. Still, even as a different man, he offered me the same stability and strength.

The detective let go of my hand and wiped my tears away. He cupped my chin and tipped my face up to look at him.

"Mason," I whispered with trembling breath, squeezing my eyes closed.

"Look at me," he insisted quietly.

Unable to ignore him, I did. He gazed down at me with sincere affection. "You and I have some long talks in front of us once we've left Charleston. But until then," he leaned in close enough so I could smell the soap on his skin.

Shivers ran down my body from the place on the top of my head where he planted his lips down to the soles of my feet. Stepping back from him in a bit of a daze, I couldn't help the goofy grin plastered on my lips.

Mason winked at me. "Now, go and find what's lost with your cousin." He left before I could process what had just happened.

I stood in the same place, staring at the spot where the detective had been standing. We definitely needed to talk so I could sort my way through whatever changes were happening between us.

A few intrusive coughs from Abigail shattered my daze. Attempting to shake off whatever confusion Mason left me with, I reminded myself of our task.

"All I can say is, wow. I've never had a man look at me like that before. Are you two together?" my cousin asked.

Her question echoed in the vast empty hall, and I cringed at the repeated question everyone, including myself, wanted to know the answer to. "We used to be. It's kind of a long story and part of the reason why I'll be relying completely on you for this."

At the reminder of needing her magic, Abigail shrunk in on herself. "I have to tell you that my abilities aren't that great. There are members of the family far more valuable than me."

I cocked an eyebrow at her. "Valuable? Does your family treat you differently depending on how well your powers work?"

Her eyes darted away, and she mumbled something under her breath about being stupid. "Don't mind me. I misspoke. Anyway, tell me what you need me to find."

Putting my questions about family dynamics to the side, I gave her the little information I knew about the missing ring. "Mason brought us here because he estimates the ring must have been lost during the commotion at the event. Also, the wardens were here searching for it."

"So, it's a ring that the woman was wearing when she died. It's not much to go on." Abigail wrung her hands together.

"I know, but we have to at least try." I stepped back to give her room.

She paced around the bottom floor and looked up at the balcony. "Maybe if I stood where she fell, I could pick up a connection."

I followed her up the stairs, my frustration rising at my inability to do things myself. By now, I'd already be on the trail, but she moved so slowly even in walking to the desired area.

When we stood in the right spot, I waited for her to do something. Her brow furrowed, and she bit her lip. "Is there something you do that's special?" she asked, delaying the process even more.

Wanting to push but not scare her, I swallowed my desire to fuss at her and gave in to the brief distraction. "It's childish, really. But when I cast spells, I like to say a little rhyme. It helps me relax and to center myself."

"Oh. That sounds nice," Abigail uttered.

Realizing she needed to do both, I offered. "Want me to give you an example?"

"Please," she exhaled with a little relief.

"I always start by closing my eyes and concentrating on the object I'm seeking," I instructed. "The rhymes seem to come to me whenever I need them, but don't worry too much. The words are really to help bring your intent into focus and give power to your spell."

"So, I could say anything?" asked Abigail.

"I think so. Here, let me show you." I closed my eyes for dramatic effect and composed on the fly. "*Within our blood, our magic flows and helps to keep us on our toes. To find the ring, please let it work, and if we're successful, Abs will twerk.*"

Fits of giggles erupted from my cousin, and I internally high-fived myself that I'd gotten her to forget her nerves. "As you can see, I tend to like things on the funny side. But maybe that was a little too zany to really focus us on anything but laughing."

Abigail wiped away the moisture around her eyes. "But I haven't found anything that funny in a long time. I get what you're trying to do, though." She caught her breath. "And for the record, I've never twerked."

"Well, we'll see what happens when we find the ring," I threatened.

She chuckled again and cracked her neck from side to side. "Okay, let's do this."

"I'll be right here if you need me," I offered, still irritated at my inability to truly help.

Taking a deep breath, she closed her eyes. After a few quiet moments, the left side of her mouth quirked up before she spoke. "*I call upon the magic power,*" she paused to think. "*To help us in our needful hour.*"

I smiled in approval, waiting to hear the rest of it.

"*Our family's magic is the thing to help us find the missing ring,*" she finished all at once, a pleased grin on her lips.

The smile faded as she concentrated. I wanted to ask her questions but feared the sound of my voice might break whatever connection she'd made.

"Okay, I'm getting the faintest sense of what we might be looking for. If I was around the person who wanted it, I could see it better. But there's definitely a faint connection," my cousin explained.

I couldn't help a question from bursting out. "What does it look like for you? Because I usually see a thread of some kind stretching out in front of me that I can tether and tie to me."

Abigail opened her eyes. "That's a really good explanation."

"I've spent a lifetime trying to explain it to others who can't experience it," I shrugged.

She gave a rueful snort. "And my life has been spent with others who expected me to do exactly what they did."

The more she slipped and revealed about our family, the more the picture of what they'd be like tarnished. Maybe I didn't really want to know what they were like.

"I'm sorry, I'm distracting you." I needed to concentrate on finding the ring, not finding where I fit in the world.

"It's okay, I've still got the connection." Abigail turned her body this way and that, facing the different directions. She pointed at the door toward the hotel. "Best I can tell, the ring is somewhere that way."

I helped her down the steps so she didn't fall and followed right behind while she walked with slow deliberate steps. When we reached the hall to the lobby, she stopped. A line of people waited in clumps by the door to the courtyard. Word about the outdoor space had made its rounds.

"There's too many people. I'm losing the connection." Abigail did her best to walk through the throng.

Worried, I rushed in front of her and tried to forge a clear path she could follow. We made it into the lobby, and she stopped again.

"Don't tell me you lost it," I begged.

A shadow crossed her face. "I'm sorry, Charli. I told you I wasn't any good."

Despite my disappointment, her lack of confidence killed me. I rubbed her arm. "Don't say that. Like you said, there's just too many people down here. Everyone's tired of being cooped up, so high emotions have to be crowding the space in here, which means it would be hard for me, too."

"You're just saying that to make me feel better." She collapsed onto a nearby couch.

I sat down next to her. "I do want you to feel better, but if anyone understands why your magic wouldn't work, it's me. Trust me."

She managed to look at me again. "I do trust you. Really. I just wanted to be able to do this for you."

"Are you giving up on me or something?" I teased, trying to ignore my disappointment. "Cheer up, Abs, I'm gonna be bugging you to try again a little later. You said it would be helpful if you could be around the person who wanted the object? Well, that person will be coming here late this afternoon. So, let's make sure you get some rest and then eat a bunch of good food to fuel our search tonight."

I stood up and offered Abigail my hand. She gripped it and let me pull her a little off balance as a joke.

"Okay, I'd be happy to try again." She paused for a moment, a wrinkle forming between her eyebrows while she considered what to say. "I hope this isn't out of line, but I wish I'd grown up knowing you."

"We can't change our past, Abs, but we can choose what to do with our present." I stopped short, too shocked at how much I sounded like Nana. "If you and I choose to, we can take it day by day and see where we end up."

She blushed a bright pink. "I'd like that."

I caught a glimpse of green hair streaking down a far hall toward the conference rooms. "If you'll excuse me, I need to go speak with someone. Like I said, rest up and prepare to conquer later."

Not wanting to lose where I saw the half-dryad rushing to, I left my cousin standing in the middle of the lobby. A cacophony of high-pitched voices rang out from behind one of the closed doors marked for employees only. I knocked on it, and an immediate silence answered.

"David, are you there?" I whispered. "Let me in."

A click of a lock alerted me to try the knob. The door opened, and I found myself staring at a supply room full of small fae, staring up at me with great fear.

One of them pointed at me with a trembling finger. "Witch."

"Don't worry, she's on our side. She's from that town I was telling you about," David reassured them. "I've got some good news to share. I've heard through our friends in the kitchen that some of the witches from this city will be coming here tonight to feed you."

I nodded without telling him I already knew that information. "Thank you for finding that out for me." Glancing around the crowded space, I decided to share my gratefulness with them all.

A tiny sprite peeked out from behind a gnome. "You talk to us like you see us."

"I do see you. And I'd be happy to talk to you anytime." I hoped they wouldn't be knocking at my door in the middle of the night, but clearly, they were all starving for normal attention.

"See, I told you she was different." David stood to his full height, pleased with himself.

The same sprite raised the toilet brush it held in her hands high in the air. "Then we will help you with whatever you need."

Agreeing cheers rose to a higher level from all of them, and I begged them to quiet down. "Remember, we don't want your bosses to know that you're helping us."

David's eyes widened. "That's right. You all need to be quieter."

I opened the door to leave, thanking them again. The half-dryad followed me out of the closet, closing the rest inside again.

"I have even better news," he exclaimed. "The two pixies, Fleet and Flit, have promised me they will give an official statement to the wardens. That means you can stop worrying about your elderly kin now."

Without thinking, I hugged David tight in absolute relief and gratitude. "Thank you. It means so much, everything you and all of the fae are doing to help."

He let his green hair cover his face to hide his embarrassment. "If I get hugs like that in Honeysuckle, I'll never leave."

"That can be arranged," I promised, preparing to walk away on a cloud of hope. "Oh, and David?"

He glanced up at me, still a little dazed from my embrace. "Yes?"

"I wasn't kidding about being careful," I warned. "The last thing I'd want is for something to happen to you because you're helping us. I don't think I could live with myself if you got hurt."

He promised to be more careful and waved for me to leave. As I turned, I heard the first of his sobs, the kind that came with relief. Knowing he didn't want me to witness him crying, I hurried down the hallway to go find Nana and tell her the good news.

Chapter Fourteen

Because Mason had already done a thorough check for listening spells and declared Nana's room clean, much to her relief, I went to her room to update her about trying to find the ring with Abigail.

"I wish Abs could have held onto the connection until we got to a less-populated area of the hotel," I complained.

"No, what you wish is that you could be the one tracking the ring instead of her. You're not foolin' anyone, Birdy, least of all me." She ruffled my hair and fetched two water bottles from the tiny fridge.

We hydrated in silence while I went down my list of things she needed to catch up on. "Oh, Tucker's doing really well in his new position. He got the wardens to include the courtyard in our borders, so now everyone can get a little sunshine."

"I knew that boy would come into his own someday. I'm just sorry it took such extreme circumstances for him to find his footing," she mused. Now, if only we could convince Leonora to step down, we might be able to assemble the strongest town council Honeysuckle's ever had."

"But wouldn't that mean Clementine would take her place?" I asked. "It would be weird to have a married couple on the council. Like it might tip the balance of power too far in their favor or something."

Nana sat down on the bed opposite me. "It wouldn't necessarily be Clementine who would take the spot. The position must be filled by a Walker, but that doesn't mean a direct descendent of the person who vacates the seat. Both you and Matt qualify because of your mother."

It wasn't the first time my grandmother tried to include me in the family legacy of keeping up the town's special protections. Pretending I could hold a position of power without the blood lineage to support me used to make me feel like I was no different than Matt. Now that I spent some time with Abigail, I couldn't help but feel a new distance from the woman who practically raised me.

"I've said this before, Nana, just Matt. Not me." I regretted my words the second they left my mouth. Why would I choose to pick at that old scab? Because my old insecurities were open and raw now that my family tree had sprouted a new branch.

"Listen here, Charlotte Vivian Goodwin." Nana held me captive with her famous glare. "You hear your last name?

Your family lines run from both the Goodwins and the Walkers."

"I'm sorry," I muttered, realizing my mistake too late.

Nana held up her hand. "No, I get it. You must be feeling a bit off kilter meeting a new person who shares your blood. But sweet honeysuckle iced tea, Birdy, she doesn't share any of the memories involving your life. She knows nothing about the bumps and scrapes and trials and tribulations that scarred you just a little bit on the outside and inside.

"She may get to share new memories and experiences with you. But your foundation in who you are today makes you a Goodwin. And your mother, who loved you to the moon and back, would absolutely support you if you took the Walker position on the town council if she was still living. I dare you to tell me differently." My grandmother crossed her arms, challenging me.

Heat rose in my cheeks, and I hated the questions swirling in my head. "Does it bother you that my biological family reached out to me? Do you think I made a mistake meeting with Abigail in the first place?"

Nana's bravado dissipated, and she placed both hands on the bed to support her as she scooted forward until our knees touched. "Birdy, look at me."

It took me digging down deep to find the courage to face her after such a question. When I did match her gaze, I noticed a mist of tears rim her eyes. My heart trembled to see her hurt.

"I'm your grandmother and you're my granddaughter.

There's nothing that will change that. I can't help but feel a little proprietary when it comes to you and your brother. First you were my son's children for me to enjoy. But too quickly, you became mine when your mother passed away. It can be hard for me to accept that you and Matt are grownups now, making your own choices." She ran her fingers through her gray hair with a sigh.

"You're not mad at me?" The simple words sounded too much like the little girl inside who'd tried all her life to earn her family's approval.

A tear trickled down her weathered cheek, and she placed both hands on my knees. "Oh, sweet bird, of course I'm not. It scares me that I don't know more about your new relatives and can't protect you from the possibility that they could hurt you. But you have every right to get to know them and make your own choices about how they fit into your life. In our family, we get to choose who's a part of it."

I launched myself at my grandmother, capturing her in my arms and telling her over and over how much I loved her. The words couldn't express how my heart would shatter if we couldn't solve the murder before they arrested her.

We both allowed ourselves to feel everything. With sniffles and snotty noses, Nana patted me on the back. "Let's pull up our big witch britches, shall we?" She wiped the moisture off her cheeks with her fingers, then did the same for me with a chuckle.

A vibrating noise and a ping interrupted our maudlin

moment, and I searched for the source. When it happened a second time, I followed the sound to the desk.

"It's coming from your purse." I picked up the leather bag and handed it to my grandmother.

She dug around for a second and pulled out her spell phone. "Frosted fairy wings, I think Lee figured out how to get these to work. I better use it quick before the local wardens catch on." Nana dismissed me with a wave of her hand.

Before I left her room, she stopped me. "Make sure you bring me back a heapin' plate of good food tonight from the potluck," she requested.

My mouth dropped. "How did you know about that?"

Nana rolled her eyes. "Haven't you figured it out by now? I know everything."

Someday, that woman would have to tell me how she always knew.

DAVID GOT word to me late in the afternoon. Like an odd game of telephone, by the time the word reached me through a gnome, who'd heard the word from a sprite, who was told by a pixie, who was sent by the half-dryad, the message got a little mixed up.

"What do you mean, 'The witches starve bears?'" I stared at the gnome, waiting for him to reveal the joke. "It doesn't make any sense."

He huffed in annoyance and started his whole explanation over again. "I told you I heard it from Trixie who was told by Fleet who was given the message from David. I'm supposed to tell you that the witches starve bears. So, now you're told." Raising his hands in the air in exasperation, the gnome left.

"What an odd guy," remarked Blythe. "And he totally got things wrong. We witches would never starve a bear or anyone else, for that matter."

"If it's a message from David, then it must have something to do with Peyton's arrival for this potluck meal." We didn't have time to decipher the mistaken code.

Lavender tapped her lip. "What if he meant the witches are here, not that we would starve a bear?"

"That works," agreed her cousin. "Plus, didn't you say he would let you know when Peyton and her crew showed up? If they're here, what do you want us to do?"

More than anything, we needed to confirm some of the gossip spread to us through the line of diminutive hotel staff. Perhaps the list of over twenty names of people who might have issues with Priscilla could be narrowed down to a smaller number.

"Right. We're Southerners, so let's do what we do best." I clapped my hands together. "Let's go down and offer to help set up. Even if they'd rather we didn't, they'll be held to their Southern upbringing and be too polite to turn us down. And then do your best to wheedle any information you can."

Preparing to go downstairs, I placed my spell phone in my pocket. It had stopped working about a half hour after Lee had gotten them to work once. He'd promised if he could make it happen for that long, then he could solve the problem. I just hoped Nana made the calls she wanted to before they gave out.

I touched the small lump under my shirt, making sure the mojo bag still hung in place. For good measure, I dabbed a little rose water on my neck. While I placed the small vial next to the one with red oil in it, I paused.

Mama Lee had explained that some of the properties of the St. John's oil had something to do with luck. Wanting to use everything I had, I took off my mojo bag from around my neck and, with great care, poured a couple of drops of the oil onto it. Nana's friend warned me not to use too much, but I really wanted to make sure things went my way tonight. Before I capped the vial, I added one more drop for good measure, and then slipped the bag over my head again and under my shirt.

Nobody needed good fortune as much as I did to get Peyton talking, and maybe the extra oomph from the Hoodoo rootwork would give me the boost I needed. If I did get lucky and all went well, I intended to complete my important mission before everyone unbuckled their belts, popped the top button of their pants open, and declared themselves full.

The four of us from Honeysuckle walked down the stairs to the floor below ours to pick up Mason and Ben. When we got close to Abigail's room, I told them I'd catch up. Abigail had said she might be able to pick up a stronger connection if she were close to a person who wanted the item. With Peyton in the hotel, we wouldn't have a better chance for her to succeed. We needed her help.

I knocked on the door and waited for an answer. Impatient, I stuck my ear to the wood and listened to see if she was there. A muffled voice that sounded like her spoke out loud, but the male voice that replied surprised me. Abigail's raised tone suggested they were arguing, but I couldn't make out specific words while eavesdropping.

Concerned and curious, I pounded on the door again. "Abs, are you okay?"

The voices on the other side stopped. After a second, my cousin called out, "Hold on a minute, please." She unlocked the door and opened it a sliver to look out. "Oh, Charli. It's you."

"Do you have a guy in there? I didn't know you had a boyfriend or significant other." I attempted to look past her, but she pulled the door tighter to her to keep me from seeing.

"No, it's just me. You must have heard the television," she explained, biting her lip.

"I guess that makes sense." My gut screamed nothing about what she was saying made sense. "And that you're okay." The terrified reflection in her eye warned me she was far from okay.

"I'm fine," Abigail lied, swallowing hard. "Is there something you wanted?"

Remembering my task, I chose to ignore my gut since I needed her help. "Some of the Charleston witches have arrived to set up a big potluck dinner for all of us stuck here in the hotel. You said your magic would work better if you had access to the person who wanted the ring. Priscilla's daughter Peyton will be the strongest candidate."

My cousin's face dropped. "And you want me to try to find the ring again. Even after my failure today."

I reached out to reassure her, but she pulled back, hiding behind the cracked opening of the door. "Fail isn't the right word. You tried and it didn't work...that time. Failure is what happens when you don't try again. And I need you to try again tonight."

Abigail squeezed her eyes shut. "I don't think it's a good idea."

"Listen, it's the best opportunity we're going to get to find that ring. If we don't grab it now, then the chances of saving my grandmother will drop drastically as the wardens will definitely make a decision soon," I explained, failing to keep the desperation out of my tone.

"Charli," Abigail protested.

"You don't know me or my background. In my family, we're not too proud to ask for help. In this situation, I'm definitely not too proud to beg for it. If you want me to get down on my knees and plead with you, I will. But I'm not leaving until you agree to help me," I stated, planting my right foot in the crack of her door so she couldn't slam it shut.

She took way longer than I thought she might to ponder my entreaty, and I considered how much it might actually hurt to get down on the floor to beg. With a resigned sigh, she nodded. "Fine. Just give me a second." Abigail tried to close the door, but my foot prevented her.

"I don't want you changing your mind and locking me out," I declared.

Her thin mouth turned up in a side grin. "You're really stubborn, you know that?"

I crossed my arms in satisfaction. "Another trait I got from my family."

Her smile faded at the word *family*, and I added her reaction to my growing list of concerns about the Wilsons. True to her word, she got ready quickly and joined me to go downstairs.

Instead of chairs laid out like we had for the first panel of the conference, the hotel staff had set up rows of tables. A few volunteers unstacked chairs from the sides of the room and distributed them around the tables. I spotted my little group from Honeysuckle helping out and engaging others in conversation. Without talking to them, I scanned the room for Peyton, but only recognized a few of the faces from yesterday. No signs of Priscilla's daughter.

A lady from behind us asked Abigail for help setting out the homemade baked goods on a nearby table. My cousin shrugged at me and obliged the request, leaving me alone in the middle of the room.

"Stand there long enough, you'll sprout roots and leaves," a familiar voice teased. Molly, the brownie who'd spoken to me on the roof, waited for me to move out of her way while she struggled under the weight of carrying a tray full of shiny serving utensils.

"Let me help," I offered.

"I've got it," the brownie insisted. "Besides, my sister would have my head if I let anyone touch these. They're Legare and Ravenel silver."

My heart quickened. I'd forgotten Molly's sister worked for Priscilla's family. If anyone had access to useful information, it would be the one who possessed intimate knowledge of the inner workings of the family.

I followed Molly to where she put down the tray. "I'm sure the hotel has lots of serving spoons and such. Why would anyone want to use their family's silver?"

The brownie huffed. "Because Peyton wanted to use the good stuff to show respect to all of you stuck in the hotel. And my sister would do anything for the darling daughter."

"Why?" I asked, tempted to dip one of the large serving ladles into a nearby steaming pot of she-crab soup.

Molly led me away from the tables and into a quiet corridor the hotel staff used. "You see, Meg's taken care of Peyton all her life. My sister treats her as if she had birthed her herself. Gave up her entire life to tend to someone who wasn't her own blood or even kind. We brownies like to stay near our families, so I tried to work in the house, too. But the way that awful woman treated those who worked for her sickened me. Meg's insistence on staying only made things worse. I took a job here at the hotel just to stay close to my sister."

I started to ask another question, but a light voice called out for Molly. "There you are. Peyton will be arriving soon, and I want everything set up just perfect for her."

Another brownie less than an inch shorter but with a face full of more wrinkles and worry than Molly approached. She glanced between the two of us and frowned.

I put on my best friendly demeanor. "You must be Meg. My name is Charli, and—"

"I know who you are, miss," the brownie cut me off. "If you would stop distracting my sister, we have much work to get done."

"Give her a chance to speak, Meg," Molly insisted. "Now that the old hag is gone, surely your loyalties won't keep you from helping."

Meg crossed her arms. "If she wants to talk to me about the family, then I have nothing to say to her."

I ignored her tactic to talk *about* me but not *to* me and took a cautious step closer. "Please. Right now, the only suspect the wardens are considering is my grandmother, and I know she didn't do it. If you have any information at all, like if there was anything you witnessed that might point us in a direction of someone else who had reason to want Priscilla gone, please share it."

The shorter brownie stood firm. "I will not be betraying the family."

"But they're not *your* family." Molly tugged on her sister's arm. "I will never understand why you stayed or why you are choosing to remain with them even now. Whatever that woman had over you to keep you in her service, she's gone. Surely, Peyton would let you go if you asked. She's nothing like that old monster was."

Meg's face softened. "No, Peyton is nothing like her mother." A strong emotion flashed in her eyes for a moment and then disappeared. "I will not divulge any family business. But I can tell you that there are other witches who would have good reason to want harm to come to my mistress's mother."

With time running out, I would take any crumb of information I could. "Can you provide names of any that might be here tonight?"

Meg's lips clammed up tight, but Molly whispered something in her ear. Softened by her sister's words, the older of the two sisters sighed. "Many of the witches were willing to send food either homemade or ordered from our local restaurants. But not as many were willing to come in person. The one who you should look for is named Frances Whitcomb."

"What can you tell me about the issues between Priscilla and her?" I pushed.

"That is for you to find out now that you have her name. I need to continue helping so that everything will be ready for Peyton." She turned to walk away and stopped. "I am sorry your family got caught up in all of this. I hope you will be able to untangle her from the web in the end."

Meg left before I could ask her anything else. Molly watched her sister walk away with deep sadness in her eyes. "I will never understand her choices. But as always, I will support her in any way I can. Good luck, Charli."

I stood in the empty corridor, wishing there were a way for me to convince Meg to give me more. Then again, I understood better than anybody what a person would do out of loyalty to family. Because of my own love for Nana, I had to let the brownie go for now and chase down the witch named Frances.

Chapter Fifteen

Mason found me when I entered the hall with the dinner preparations in full swing. "Where were you?"

I told him about my conversation with the two brownies and asked if he had any ideas about finding Frances. He surveyed the activity buzzing around us.

I tried to stop him when he picked up a tinfoil covered platter. He approached another person walking by and spoke to them, pointing at the stolen food he was holding. When they finished talking, he waited for a beat and set the tray back down.

"Come on." Grabbing my hand, he dragged me out another door that led outside.

We spotted the behind of a woman wiggling as she rummaged through the backseats of an expensive car. When she extracted herself and stood up, I found myself staring at Frances Whitcomb, the woman who had helped moderate the first panel and one of the top names from the list.

"Oh, good. I'm glad they sent help. I've got several containers full of food in the back of my car to bring in and only my two hands." She smiled in relief.

Mason approached with purpose. "We'd be glad to assist you." He flashed me a knowing glance.

Frances stuck her head back in the car. "So, where are y'all from?" she tittered from inside.

Mason shot an uncertain look at me, and I fought to come up with a quick lie. "Um, we both live in Cricket Creek. About a two-and-a-half hours drive northwest from here."

"I'll bet you're tired of being cooped up in here. But from what I hear, things should be over real soon and y'all can head on home," she revealed.

A rustling behind us caught my attention, and I found a warden sitting next to the side entrance in a chair, munching on a brownie he must have snagged from inside and reading his phone. Mason and I tried not to be noticed while we waited for Frances.

She pulled out a large roasting pan and handed it to Mason. "I didn't cook all of this, in case you're wondering. Some of the ladies were willing to contribute but didn't want to return to the hotel until they arrest the person responsible for Prissy's death."

My fingers curled into fists, and Mason bumped me with his hip to keep me steady. I took the next aluminum foil-covered pan from her and resisted the urge to dump the hot contents down the entire front of her dress.

"The word is," she kept going, pulling out a smaller dish and setting it on top of the one I held, "that they think they already have the murderer here."

"Really?" I glared at her, gritting my teeth to stop myself from saying more.

Frances straightened all of a sudden. "Oh my goodness, what if that person ends up in that room, eating our food? Is it legal to feed a murderer?" She bent down to sort through the other dishes.

"I don't know, have you fed yourself today?" I mumbled.

"Shh," Mason hissed beside me.

Frances pulled herself out of her car. "What was that?"

Plastering on a smile, I amped up my Southern accent. "I was just conversin' with my friend here about the rumors that have been going around. I heard that the lady who died deserved it. That a lot of people didn't like her."

She balanced two smaller dishes, one in each hand, and closed the car door with her foot. "That's a terrible thing to say," she scolded. We headed back inside, and once we got into the hall, Frances slowed down. "Although, truth be told, I think our entire witch community will be better off without Prissy."

"Why's that?" pushed Mason. "Here, stack that second dish on top of mine so you don't have to carry as much."

"Thank you, sugar." Frances beamed at the detective. Looking around her, she leaned in and whispered loud enough for us to hear, "I hate to speak ill of the dead, but she had a pretty nasty side to her underneath her veneer of perfection. She always got what she wanted, no matter who her heels had to step on to get it."

"Hmm." It took hardly any prompting to keep her talking.

"Like, I didn't want to do anything for the conference other than volunteer behind the scenes," she admitted as if the job had been strenuous. "But Prissy asked me to moderate that first panel for her. And refusing was out of the question because...oh, look at me, prattling on. Let's set these down and go back for more."

On our second round, once we were out of earshot of the others, Frances continued to tell us other of Priscilla's transgressions. Since she no longer had the woman's proverbial stiletto heel on her back, her newfound freedom loosened her wagging tongue.

While she pulled out the last dishes from her car, I found a break in the conversation to turn things around and shine the light back on her. "It sounds as if you could understand that someone who had a considerable reason to hate Priscilla could be her killer. If you had to guess, who would you say did it?"

Frances stopped digging around in her car and stood straight. Her face sobered. "I wouldn't presume to guess. You can take those dishes inside now."

I took a step forward, closing her in against her own vehicle. "Come on, surely there's been talk. Who does everyone think is the murderer?"

"I-if you believe what they're saying, then it's the lady who was on the panel with Prissy. The one from Honeysuckle Hollow," she stammered. Her eyes darted over to where the warden had been sitting and found the seat empty.

"Why? What grudge did she hold against Priscilla that would spur her to kill?" I handed off the dish in my hand to Mason. "Her only issue was when Priscilla's brother overstepped his reach from your town's witches' council and tried to take over her town. But that was all settled and done with."

In my frustration, a little power erupted to life in me, and sparks flowed down my arms and danced on the tips of my fingers.

"Charli," Mason warned.

"You're not from Cricket Creek, are you?" Frances squeaked.

"No," I stated. "And you had more reason than most to hate Priscilla Ravenel Legare, didn't you, Ms. Whitcomb? And now that she's gone, so is her treatment of you, right?"

Her eyes widened until the whites of them almost swallowed the rest. "Fine. Yes, I hated her. Please don't hex me," she pleaded.

Realizing how far I'd gone, I breathed in a cleansing breath and released my anger. The sparks faded and I held up my hands to show her my good intentions.

"I wouldn't have done anything." I tried to believe myself so she wouldn't hear a lie. "But I think you need to admit the truth. That you had more than enough reasons to hate

Priscilla, including a fight you had with her a couple of months ago at an event here at the Hyperion Hall."

Frances's eyes narrowed. "How did you know that?"

I cringed at my mistake, and Mason continued the conversation. "What happened to cause the argument?"

The woman slouched against the side of her car in defeat. "She found out I'd been supporting the other side, talking to those who were looking for ways to change how things ran with us here in Charleston a while back. She threatened to ostracize me in every way possible."

"Why didn't you just leave Charleston?" I asked. "That seems like a simple solution if you didn't like her leadership."

"Because my family has been here for generations. My husband's family goes back to the city's founding. I want my children to live here." Frances sniffed. "My pride kept me from walking away. That night of the event a couple of months ago, I attempted to back her off of her threats by making one of my own."

I lifted my eyebrow. "You tried to play her at her own game. Using what ammunition?"

Frances shook her head and pursed her lips. "I think I'm done talking. I don't know how you knew about our argument, but now that Prissy's dead, it doesn't matter anymore."

With one last effort to get her to understand, I attempted to appeal to her sympathies. "Ms. Whitcomb, you said you didn't like how Priscilla ran things or how she treated people. Well, the person they're trying to pin her murder on is the absolute opposite. She stays our leader because she protects her people, not because she tries to stay on top by destroying them."

The hardened expression on her face morphed to one of regret. "Then whoever she leads is very lucky to have her."

"Well, we won't for much longer unless the real killer is found." Unable to stop myself, I pushed harder. "Frances, I've heard from more than one source you had ample reasons to do it."

The woman's eyes widened in fear. "But I didn't. I swear it. Sure, I wanted someone to finally stand up to the old witch and take over. But I could never take another person's life. Whoever is saying otherwise is lying."

"Or you are." I watched her face to catch her reaction to my bold accusation.

She tilted her head to regard someone behind us, and Mason and I spotted the warden returning to his seat with a plate full of food. Frances cleared her throat. "Unless you have proof to have him come over here and arrest me, I suggest you go back inside."

I held up my hands in surrender to keep her from involving the warden. "Then consider this. Whoever did commit the murder is willing to let an innocent woman take the blame. That person, even if they killed for a good reason, would be no better than Priscilla in the long run, willing to sacrifice someone else's life for their own gain."

Mason and I left her to ponder my words. I stomped inside, not caring if the warden took notice of me. "I'm guessing she didn't share enough for us to convince anyone she'd be a good suspect?" I asked the detective.

"Other than having an argument with the lady, unless there's evidence of Priscilla's treatment or the being who witnessed the argument is willing to come forward, then it's all speculation. Hearsay." He placed a hand on my shoulder. "I think you should focus on talking to Peyton and finding the ring."

We entered the room full of tables and found the new woman in charge directing things like an experienced ringleader at a circus. She commanded authority and looked remarkably like her mother at the helm of the ship, except Peyton wore a genuine smile of appreciation rather than calculation. Meg stood right by her side, making sure those who took the requests fulfilled them.

Checking her tablet, Peyton called out her orders. "Let's put the pots of she-crab soup on the table with ladles and cups. Move the dessert table to the far end there on the left so it's not in the middle of the buffet line. Can someone check with the chef at Magnolias to see if they can add their yummy fried green tomato and pimento cheese canapés to their order? They should be bringing in mini waffles and fried chicken bites, too."

I elbowed Mason. "We need to find the ring and fast. My stomach might crawl out of me in rebellion if I don't eat some of what smells so delicious."

Meg caught sight of me watching Peyton and narrowed her dark beady eyes. She pursed her lips in displeasure, and I doubted whether or not we'd be able to get within a foot of Priscilla's daughter.

Peyton stopped directing the chaos and looked up. When she caught sight of me, she stopped what she was doing. Pointing with her manicured finger, she called out, "You." Her smile faded.

Swallowing hard, I gestured at Mason, hoping to change her intended target. She shook her head, refusing my alternative. "No, you. We need to talk."

Chapter Sixteen

P eyton stopped pointing and curled her finger, gesturing for me to come to her. Mason didn't leave my side, and I approached in a less confident manner than I intended. Meg glared at me the whole time, her protective gaze burning a hole in me.

"Yes?" I hated the meekness in my voice.

"I was told you know something about a ring," she accused.

Holy unicorn horn, how did she know? "Who told you that?" I blinked my eyes, feigning innocence.

"I did," Abigail stepped out from nearby. "Weren't you telling me that you heard someone say they found a ring at the Hyperion Hall last night?"

I couldn't believe my cousin would rat me out like that. My mouth gaped open as her betrayal hit me.

Mason's head nodded up and down in an exaggerated fashion. "Yes, I remember you saying that lost ring was found."

He bumped my hip with his and Abigail widened her eyes for me to pick up on the ruse. I prevented myself from smacking my forehead at my slowness on picking up the clues.

"Oh, right. The ring." I addressed Peyton with more confidence. "Are you looking for it?"

Her shoulders dropped and she sighed with relief. "Yes. Oh, Meg, did you hear that? I think they found Mother's ring."

"Yes, that would be a good thing, Miss Peyton." Meg tried to sound happy, but her body language betrayed her.

Priscilla's daughter gushed, completely oblivious to the brownie's trepidation of us, "You are a savior. It's belonged to the Ravenel's for generations, and it was supposed to come to me."

Abigail moved to stand behind Peyton, mouthing words at me. She pointed at her ring finger, and said with no sound, "What kind?"

"Right," I declared, answering her out loud by mistake. "I mean, right, it sounds like an important piece of jewelry. It was a gold ring with a sapphire surrounded by a circle of small diamonds, if I heard correctly."

Peyton's face dropped. "No, the family's ring was platinum and had an emerald flanked by two diamonds."

Meg raised an eyebrow in suspicion. "It sounds like you heard about someone else's ring instead."

Abigail gave me an excited thumbs up from behind Peyton's back. When Priscilla's daughter turned around, my cousin pretended to inspect an invisible mark on her hand to cover up her gesture.

"I appreciate you organizing this dinner. The hotel food isn't bad, but your potluck is a nice change for us." I left out Tucker's part in convincing her to put the whole thing together, allowing her all the credit.

"I understand how inconvenient it all is. I'm not liking what I'm hearing about your grandmother either. I told the chief that she was nowhere near my mother when she collapsed. Isn't it horrible, Meg?" She took my hand in hers, rubbing the back of my skin with her thumb in sympathy.

Either she truly believed in Nana's innocence or she could manipulate people with as much mastery as her mother had. "And I'm truly sorry for your loss. You are incredible to be helping all of us when you should be in mourning."

"Mother wouldn't have wanted that. 'Keep up appearances,' she'd say. No matter what, things always had to look like they were going right." Peyton cast her eyes down. "I shouldn't say things like that. Awful words have been coming out of my mouth ever since..." she trailed off.

Meg stopped protecting the young woman from us and wrapped her arms about her middle. "There, there, Miss Peyton."

Abigail tilted her head, indicating we should go, but I didn't want to leave the grieving daughter without offering some comfort. "I've lost both of my parents. It'll take time until your life balances out again. And don't even hope for a return to what it used to be."

"I don't think I want it to go back." Peyton sniffed, patting Meg on the back and pushing her away. "But I hope when I move forward, things will get a little better."

"Give it time." Meg gazed at Peyton with admiration and a deep love. Perhaps that strong emotion explained why she would never leave the family despite Molly's insistence.

Peyton rolled her shoulders back and grinned, although the smile didn't reach her eyes. "I'll get through it. We all will. Now, if y'all want to fix yourselves some plates early while we've got a little bit of everything, I swear I won't report you to the authorities."

I attempted to laugh but only managed a weird chortle. Thanking her, I walked away with Abigail and Mason, acting as normal as I could. We made it to a corner outside the room before I had to almost squeal from how close I thought we'd come to getting caught.

"How did you come up with the idea to get the detail of the rings?" I asked Abigail, surprised to find my cousin had some tricks up her sleeves.

Words tumbled out of my cousin in her excitement. "I didn't know where you and Mason disappeared to, and I knew you'd want to talk to her at some point to try and pull the information out of her. Tricking her into thinking a ring had been found was the only idea that came to mind."

"It was a great idea," Mason admitted. "Can you work with the details she revealed?"

A little pride leaked into Abigail's expression. "Having an idea of what it looks like is great. I can work from that. But since I wanted things to be a little stronger this time, I nabbed these to seal the spell." She held up a couple strands of Peyton's ice blonde hair.

"Way to go, Abs." Without her permission, I flung myself at my cousin and hugged her hard. When her hands wrapped around my body, I finally felt like we understood each other on a different level.

"I'll leave you both to it again and go check on the rest of our gang to see what they've found out." Mason winked at Abigail, making her blush. He ran a finger down my arm, causing goosebumps to break over my skin.

My cousin watched him leave. "I think the two of you should be together. There's a strong connection between you."

"If you help me find the ring, then we'll stay up tonight to have our first sleepover together, and I'll give you the whole scoop. In the meantime, I can give you some space to work up your spell," I offered.

"I've got a better idea." She held out her hand. "Let's try to work this together. It might boost the magic."

My stomach dropped, and I hated repeating what she already knew. "I told you, my powers aren't working right now."

"Or maybe you need a little boost yourself. Come on. I've even composed a rhyme." She wiggled her fingers.

A little charmed by her change in spirit and excitement, I

accepted her hand. "Fine. I just hope I don't drag you down like an anchor."

"Now who needs to stop acting like they've already failed? I have faith in you, Charli." She gripped me a little harder. "Don't laugh at my spell."

We both closed our eyes, and I waited for her spellcasting to start, trying to focus on supporting her rather than wallowing in jealousy.

Abigail took a deep breath and concentrated. "*I call on our magic through our lifeblood bond and bind it with hair from the snow-white blonde. Seek out the treasure, an emerald ring, to help out Charli's kin, her freedom to bring.*"

I swore I felt a little tingle flow from my cousin into me when she activated her spell. Not wanting to lose it, I attempted to picture the ring in my mind and tested myself to see if I could feel any connection. A slight wave of power flowed through me, but I couldn't detect a thread or anything.

"Do you sense anything?" Abigail asked me.

"Just your magic, I think. Why? Have you picked up on something?"

My cousin squeezed my hand. "Open your eyes, Charli." She waited for me. "Can you truly not feel the connection?"

I checked my gut again but came up empty. "No. Maybe I should let you do this on your own."

She gripped me harder. "No, I was only wondering. Here, I'm going to tether the connection to me so I won't lose it." Staring off in front of her, she furrowed her brow in concentration. "There."

The second she declared the connection tied, I felt it and a faint golden thread stretched in front of her. "When you see whatever it is you tethered to yourself, what does it look like?"

"I think you described it well. Like a glowing thread or thin rope. When I bond with it, it pulls me toward it. Like now." She pointed in the direction I saw the link.

A mix between a chuckle and a sob gushed out of me. I covered my mouth with my free hand to stop myself from losing it.

"You see it now, don't you?" Happiness radiated off of my cousin and warmed me down to my bones.

I could only nod. Swallowing back my tears of joy, I lifted my chin. "Let's go find it."

We walked through the lobby toward the elevators. Whoever had the ring held it somewhere upstairs. Too many people used the elevators to come down to the potluck, so we navigated the stairs, still grasping onto each other. Walking up the stairs in tandem proved more awkward as we passed each floor. The connection beckoned us onto the second to last floor.

Abigail stopped moving and jerked me back. She stood next to the decorative table with a decaying bouquet of flowers in the middle of the hall next to the elevators and stairwell.

"I think I'm wrong. We should stop here and try again later." She attempted to pull her hand away from mine.

I held on tighter. "No. I can tell we're getting close." I

gestured to the hall to our right. "It's clear as day to me that someone has it in a room down there."

"I'm stopping whether you want me to or not." Abigail let the hairs drop from her other hand and pulled out of my grip.

The golden thread wavered and disappeared. All sense of the tracking magic died. "Why'd you do that?" I exclaimed, anger and disappointment cooling the bond I thought we'd forged.

"You don't want to find the ring. Trust me, Charli, it'll lead you down the wrong path. Let's find another way to prove your grandmother's innocence." She backed away from me.

"I don't understand you." I closed the distance between us, trying to get her to see reason. "One second you want to help, the next, you try to run away. What is it you're not telling me?"

"Nothing."

"Then let's finish this. Please." Without hesitation, I got on my knees. "I haven't experienced that magic in so long and we were so close. Please don't stop now. Please." The last plea came out in a trembling whisper.

Large tears poured down Abigail's face. "I knew I would end up hurting you. I always disappoint everyone."

She held out her hand, and I took it, grateful she'd changed her mind. Helping me to my feet, she bit her lip and looked away.

"Cast the spell again," I commanded.

Abigail squeezed me one more time and let me go. "No. I won't be the one."

"You're not making any sense. If you won't do it, by all the gods, I will." I closed my eyes and did my best to push down my anger and focus my intent.

"Trust me, Charli. Don't do it." Abigail held up her hands in surrender when I glared at her.

Wanting the extra luck, I pulled the mojo bag out from under my shirt and clutched it while I spellcast. "*I have no time to stop and fight, bring back my power and make it right. No more in darkness shall I wait to fully accept and embrace my fate. The tracking magic to me I bind, and with it, an emerald ring I'll find.*"

Like a lightbulb flickering on and off, the same connection from before appeared and disappeared in front of me. "I can still see it's nearby."

Unable to capture it and tie it to me, I could only follow the unsteady path it blazed with slow steps. When the connection guttered and winked out of existence, it broke the spell, and I leaned over, gasping to catch my breath.

The door opened, and a pair of painted toes came into view. "Did you bring me some food, Birdy?"

Chapter Seventeen

I straightened and faced the one person I hadn't anticipated seeing.

Nana glanced between Abigail and me. "What's going on?"

My cousin stood a few feet back, her face crestfallen. "I told you to let it go. I wish you would have trusted me." She turned and raced off down the hall.

My grandmother took a step out of her room, holding her door open with her foot. "What just happened?"

When my wits returned, I panicked and ushered her back inside. Once we were alone in private, I grabbed onto both of her arms. "You know about the ring that Peyton asked the wardens to find? The one her mother was probably wearing the night of her murder?"

Nana listened with keen interest. "Ben filled me in. Let me

guess. They think whoever killed Priscilla took the ring. Find it and they'll find the murderer. Sounds like lazy investigating."

"No, sounds like a perfect way to set someone up to blame." I moved about her room, searching for places where the piece of jewelry might have been planted.

My grandmother caught on fast. "You and Abigail were tracking the ring, weren't you?" Without waiting for an answer, she cracked a tiny grin. "You got your powers back."

She had promised me my magic would return at some point if I would be patient. I think after so many months had passed, even she had lost a little of her faith. Although I would love to take her up on the offer to throw me one of her famous parties to celebrate, we first had to make sure she made it back to Honeysuckle at all.

"Yes, but ignore that. Abigail figured out where the ring was before I did. And the connection I managed to make with it brought me to your door. Now that my cousin has run off, I have no idea where the thing is hidden since you haven't discovered it on your own." I opened drawers of the dresser and rooted around Nana's clothing.

"Whoever set this up wouldn't have wanted me to find it, so they would have placed it in a less obvious setting." She ran her fingers over the top of a framed print of a Charleston scene, managing to only wipe dust off it.

"This is going to take us forever. Let me at least try to make my magic work again." I closed my eyes, concentrating harder than normal, and mumbled a spell under my breath. A couple of tingles rushed down my arms and into my fingers, but the power dissipated like smoke in the air. "I don't think I can do it again."

We checked every single surface in the room, under every piece of furniture, and removed all of Nana's clothing from the drawers until we'd both gone behind each other three times with no success. In a matter of several flustered moments, we'd destroyed the room.

"Maybe your senses were wrong," my grandmother suggested.

My anger at my cousin flared. "I don't think so. She knew exactly where the tracking powers would lead us. She'd been cagey off and on about helping, but now I'm sure she knows way more than she's let on. In fact, let me contact Mason to have him detain her." I took my spell phone out of my pocket.

"I know you're angry with her right now," Nana started. "But be careful how you handle her. You don't know her side of the story and it would be a shame for you to burn your bridges with her out of a misunderstanding."

"Frosted fairy wings, the spell phones are blocked again." I tossed mine on the bed. "At least the wards will keep her in. Unless she sneaks out when the dinner is over and the Charleston crew packs up to leave again."

"Then that will be her choice to live with." Nana surveyed the mess we'd made. "We should clean things up and see if maybe the ring presents itself while we reorganize."

I picked up one of her shirts I'd flung on the bed and

folded it into a tight rectangle. "I just don't want the wardens to appear right when we find it."

Something rattled in the room. Nana and I stopped what we were doing and stood still, listening. When nothing else happened, we let our held breaths go and got back to cleaning.

"The wardens are going to do what they are going to do. You can't control their actions, only how we react to them. I've been prepared for them to march through that door and arrest me without a stitch of evidence."

The sound of something metal clinking against glass interrupted us again. I dropped the piece of clothing I was folding and stepped over a strewn pillow on the floor. Nana paced in front the dresser, her head cocked to the side to listen. She held her finger up to her mouth to indicate for me to remain quiet. A strained silence followed except for the pounding of my racing heart in my ears.

My grandmother gazed at her reflection in the mirror for long seconds. I wanted to ask her why her appearance mattered at a time like this, but kept my mouth shut, obeying her request.

"Could it be as simple as that?" she wondered out loud. Holding her hands in front of her, she moved them over the surface of the mirror, not touching it, but skimming as close as she could. "Yes, I think they did."

"Did what?" I asked.

Nana closed her eyes and dropped one hand, moving her dominant one over the surface in a meticulous side-to-side pattern until she stopped in the left-hand corner. "There. That's where someone has hidden the ring."

The mirror reflected her pointed finger back at her but showed no sign of the jewelry. "I don't understand."

My grandmother stood back and scoffed. "It's old magic. Something not taught anymore because it can be incredibly unreliable. Mirrors and mirrored surfaces used to be used in all manners. Witches would use them to scry, to communicate with each other long before we had telephones, and as a place to hide very valuable things."

"And you think someone has used the mirror to hide the ring? Who would have done that?" I closed the distance between us to inspect the mirror for myself. The only thing it revealed to me was the wrinkle creased between my eyebrows.

She pushed me to the side and flourished her hands in front of the mirror a couple of times. When nothing appeared, I doubted my grandmother's guess.

"I think it's spellcast to reveal the hidden object when the right word or words are spoken." Nana raised her hand to the side of her mouth and spoke in a clear, loud voice. "The wardens are coming to arrest me."

The same tinkling noise from before rattled louder and louder, and my grandmother indicated the same spot in the lower left-hand corner of the mirror. "See? It's in there, but whoever cast the spell either didn't do it right or my protection spell I performed on the room after Mason cleared it of any bugs has corrupted it. Let me see if I can get it out of there."

Before she could perform any of her strong magic, I tugged on her sleeve. "Maybe you should leave it in there. I mean, if we can't get it out, then the ring may never be found. And then whoever was trying to use it to make sure the wardens arrested you for Priscilla's murder, might come back to try and retrieve it."

The ring jangled and clinked inside the looking glass, still unable to extract itself despite me repeating the key words that called the piece of jewelry forth.

"If we had more time, then your idea might be the better one so we could find out who's a part of my framing," Nana acquiesced. "But I'll bet the chief makes his move tomorrow morning. I'd rather take possession of the ring and get ahead of the problem rather than trying to ignore it and hope it didn't break itself free at the wrong time, making me look guiltier than ever."

I opened my mouth to argue with her but thought better of it. In all my years trusting Nana, I couldn't come up with a good reason to stop doing so now. With great interest, I watched her address the mirror.

Raising her hand in front of the spot, she spoke out loud, "*Magus Revelo.*"

If I hadn't been looking at the right spot, I would have missed the minuscule thin lines that crackled over the area with a faint glow like a spider web.

"It's being stubborn. Either my protection spell was too good or whoever placed the ring in my mirror knew the words but not how to fully pull the trick off. Let me try something else." She rolled her shoulders and held up both hands in front of the mirror. "*Manifesto Speculus Arcanus*."

The web of cracks radiated brighter until the reflective surface broke and shards of the mirror scattered on the dresser. A dark hole stretched beyond the room behind it. With great care, Nana reached her hand inside until her arm disappeared up to her armpit.

"Yeah, whoever attempted this wasn't an expert. I think there's something here, if I can just reach...got it!" She withdrew her arm, being extra careful not to cut herself on the rough edges of glass.

Uncurling her fingers, she displayed the object in the middle of her palm. The green of the large emerald between two diamonds sparkled despite not having any special light on it.

"That's what Peyton described," I exclaimed, a little taken back at the beauty of the piece of jewelry.

My grandmother picked it up and held it between her fingers. "There's an inscription inside it. It says, "*Pence pour moi*." My French is rusty, but I think that means, 'Think of me.' It makes sense that it belongs to the Ravenel family since their ancestors who established the city came from France." She turned the ring around, inspecting it.

"Now that we've found it, we have to get rid of it or hide it." I reached out to take it from her, but she snatched it away.

"We are not going to obstruct justice," Nana scolded. "The only reason we know that the ring is in anyway connected to

Priscilla is because Ben took illegal pictures of the case file. Otherwise, it's considered a lost item and it should be turned in."

I held out my hand, palm up. "No, Peyton told me about it, so Ben's off the hook. Give it to me and let me claim I found it somewhere else. If the wardens hear you had anything to do with it, they'll arrest you faster than you can say *unicorn manure*."

My grandmother hesitated. "I don't think that's a wise idea. I mean, it's kind of cheating."

"They're cheating, Nana!" My raised voice alarmed her, and I did my best to stay as calm as possible. "If things were fair, then they would have launched a full-on investigation, finding out all the information we've worked our behinds off to gather. If they're not going to play by the rules, then we have to change them. And you were the one who told me to blow out the wall behind me if I got stuck."

She narrowed her eyes at me. "Don't use my words against me."

"Give me the ring."

Excessive pounding on the door interrupted our discussion. Nana called out, "Hold on one moment, please."

A man's voice spoke through the closed entrance. "Ms. Goodwin, this is Deputy Warden Jones. Please open your door."

"Pixie poop," I whispered.

Nana held up the ring in front of her. "I'll bet there was a warning hex on the ring. As soon as we activated it, even though it was stuck in the mirror, it somehow summoned the wardens here."

"Put it back in the mirror," I insisted, pointing at the broken surface.

She shook her head. "No, that's tampering with the evidence. Maybe they'll believe our story."

"And maybe pigs will fly right by the window right... about...now. See? No pigs. Hide the ring," I pleaded.

The deputy banged on the door. "Ms. Goodwin, I can lawfully open this by force if necessary."

My grandmother instructed me to answer him while she stood by the mirror in order not to disturb the scene any more than she needed to. As soon as he gained entrance, the deputy surveyed the mess.

Without asking one question, he held up his hand in front of him, allowing a little power to spark to life. "Both of you, put your hands in the air."

Disgusted and angry, I kept my eyes on the deputy but spoke to my grandmother. "Hey, Nana?"

"Yeah, Birdy?" she replied, not moving a muscle.

I hated with all of my heart that the young warden had proven me right. "Unicorn manure."

Chapter Eighteen

Chief Huxley appeared in the doorway with another warden in tow. He entered the room, a smug smile plastered on his face. "Looks like y'all have done a real number in here. It could make our job harder unless you cooperate."

With my hands still raised in the air, I tried to block his view of Nana. He warned me off and gestured with his hand for me to back away. Instead of obeying right away, I turned to check with my grandmother first.

"It's all right, Birdy. Trust me." My faith had been tested a lot this evening, and the presence of the wardens didn't help. In utter reluctance, I took a step back to give the chief a clear path to address my grandmother.

"Now, Ms. Goodwin, are we going to have a problem?" He stood a good four inches taller than Nana and used his height to attempt to intimidate her. When she didn't give him the reaction of fear he sought, his smile dropped. "Show me what's in your hand."

"Don't," I cried out.

"You keep quiet." The chief waved two fingers at me. "That's your second warning. If I have to address you a third time, I will have Deputy Jones remove you from the room."

My hands shook, and I clenched them into fists to steady myself and keep him from seeing the fear racing through me. My brain raced through any possible way to get us out of the situation, considering Nana's thoughts about blowing out the wall behind us when we're cornered. Other than actually spellcasting an exploding bomb hex, I couldn't find a way out except to cooperate.

"I'm going to ask you again to show me what you have clenched in that hand of yours," Chief Huxley demanded.

Nana lowered her right arm, and the two younger wardens got a little twitchy. They rushed closer and held up their hands, ready to blast her with their powers. Their boss backed them off with a few words.

Turning her hand, my grandmother unclenched her fist and revealed the ring laying in the palm of her hand. The emerald flashed green in the light, and if it didn't have a connection to Priscilla, I might think it truly beautiful.

"That's what I thought you might be trying to conceal," the chief said.

"I wasn't the one hiding anything. I found it in my room,"

Nana replied with a calmness that only I understood reflected how much she held back her anger.

The chief didn't know he stood in the eye of a storm, and if he took a step out of line, he'd find out fast how much power and fury my grandmother could rain down on him if she so chose.

Chief Huxley lowered his chin so he could look down his nose at her. "Lady, don't pee on my leg and tell me it's rainin'! First, when you spoke to us at the station, you claimed you had been in the bathroom upstairs and had not approached or threatened Ms. Priscilla nor been the cause of her untimely death. You just happened to show up immediately after she collapsed in the hall."

"That's correct," Nana replied.

"Yet you don't deny some of the reports from other witnesses that earlier in the day after some panel, you were overheard saying in the hotel lobby that you wanted to fight her until only one of you was standing." The chief played a tighter game than I'd expected.

I opened my mouth to explain what she'd meant at the time, but Nana flashed me a look to keep me quiet. "As I said at the station, you can't take the comment out of context. It was said in frustration after Priscilla verbally attacked our town as retribution for her brother's failed attempt to take over Honeysuckle Hollow."

The chief scratched his balding head. "It seems to me if your town produces criminals, then maybe it needs overseeing by a better organization."

A snort burst out of me, and the chief shot me a side glance of death. Pretending I sneezed, I wiped my finger under my nose and waited for him to finish.

"Now I find you in possession of a ring the daughter claims her mother would never take off. Why would you have the object if you hadn't been involved in the murder?" asked the chief.

"I've already told you, I found the ring in my room. I had nothing to do with it being here. My granddaughter can corroborate that." Nana continued standing with her open hand in front of him, the key piece of evidence still in her palm.

"It's true," I interjected. "Someone used a spell to hide the ring within the mirror." With one finger, I pointed at the corner that was broken to retrieve the piece of jewelry.

The chief shuffled over to inspect the broken shards. "Looks like a regular broken mirror. Bad luck for you. It's been a while since I've heard of anyone using that old trick. Takes some know how they don't teach anymore."

"Well, I'm no spring chicken," Nana replied, a little of her normal snark sneaking back into her tone.

"Therefore, you could have been the one to hide it in the first place," the chief accused.

"*Could* doesn't mean I did, sir. And if I had hidden it in a place you say nobody would think to look, why would I break it out of said hiding spot for you to find me with it?" Nana turned the chief's game back on him with her logic.

He stroked his mustache, considering her words. Having

been on the other side of my grandmother's debating skills, I hoped he'd give up his attack, take the ring, and leave her alone.

"Furthermore," my grandmother continued. "You've got some trackers stuck here at the hotel with you. If you engaged them, they might be able to use the ring to figure out who took it in the first place."

He frowned. "How do you know there are trackers here?"

Nana tipped her head in my direction. "My granddaughter is one."

Clearly, my grandmother had more faith in my magic returning than I did. Yes, I made it work once, but I had no guarantees it would happen again. Assuming the role as one of Nana's pieces in her game, I nodded in affirmation.

The chief chortled. "Like I would believe your granddaughter wouldn't lie for you."

"There is another witch with tracking abilities here you could use," Nana suggested, leaving out the part about Abigail's loose connection to me.

I had no desire to engage my cousin in using her talents again. Not until I got to the bottom of what she knew and why things had suddenly gone all pear-shaped with her.

Chief Huxley dismissed my grandmother. "Forget using trackers. The evidence was found in your possession. Add that to the previous statements about your hostile comments and your lack of evidence to prove where you were prior to the death, then—"

"Wait, Chief," I interrupted. "There is someone who is

willing to testify that Nana was where she said she was. In the bathroom. Two someone's, actually."

Nana raised her eyebrows while the head warden frowned in consternation. "That sounds too convenient to me, miss. Exactly who are these witnesses you say are willing to give a statement?"

I lowered my hands for the first time, allowing the blood to rush back into them. "Fleet and Flit. I think they work in the laundry for the hotel."

The chief sneered. "Fleet and Flit? Those don't sound like proper names."

"They're pixies," I explained. "And before you make a mistake, I suggest you find them and hear what they have to say. In fact, it would be a good idea if you interviewed several of the hotel staff. You might find there's more than just one person who could have had issues with your grand dame."

One of the wardens stepped up. "Chief, I could go take statements."

"Quiet, Hollins," his boss barked. "I'm the one in charge here."

One of the wardens' radios crackled to life, and a muffled voice called out an intelligible message. The warden answered but couldn't understand what was being said through all the static.

"Give it here," demanded the chief. "This is Huxley. We can't understand you. Repeat the message."

More static garbled the voice on the other side. One clear word made it through. "Emergency."

"Jones, Hollins, you two go down and—"

Another warden arrived breathless from exertion. "Chief, we've got a situation down in the basement."

Chief Huxley swore under his breath. "Then take these two with you and get it under control."

The young woman shook her head. "You don't understand. There are two dead bodies down there, and all of the fae hotel staff are ready to stage a revolt. We're stretched to the max to keep things from getting out of hand."

The chief growled his displeasure and regarded Nana and me. "Fine. Bring these two down with us."

"Are they under arrest, sir?" the new warden asked.

The chief's face changed from frustration to revelation. "Not yet. In fact, this may work out better. After we deal with the help, then we can arrest her in front of the others. That will show everybody here how we keep order in our city."

Nana rolled her eyes. "Chief?"

"What?" he bellowed.

She waved her hand holding the ring in front of him. Snatching it away from her, he pocketed it and stomped out of the room. Nana followed behind him escorted by the warden who'd volunteered to take statements about the two new deaths.

"Everyone will be happy when the ward is lifted," stated Deputy Jones, waving his hand for me to walk in front of him.

"I will be happiest when justice is served," I retorted. The tiny shove in my back to get me moving conveyed the warden's displeasure.

Tense silence filled the elevator all the way down to the basement floor. As soon as the doors slid open, we entered into bedlam. Multiple voices rose in anger, and a line of wardens kept their hands in front of them, using their power to hold back the crowd.

In between the two groups lay two small bodies, crumpled in a disjointed pile. My heart dropped at the sight of Flit and Fleet's lifeless forms. The brother and sister deserved much better than having their lives taken.

The chief stared at the chaos, uncertain how to handle it. "I don't understand. They shouldn't be able to fight our warden power like that."

Nana's mouth curved with a slight grin. "If I were you, I might try talking to them rather than treating them like animals you have to control."

"I'll be the judge of that," the chief grumbled. Facing the growing problem, he watched as his force was losing to a pack of angry fae. "Jones, Hollins, get in there. You two," he pointed at my grandmother and me. "Don't even think about moving."

Left to stand together, I watched the additional wardens attempt to hold the horde back with concern. "Why does this scene please you?" I asked my grandmother.

"It doesn't. I'm mortified, but I'm also relieved to see the wardens struggle," Nana whispered back. "It means things are coming to an end."

I hated when she got cryptic with me. "What do you mean?"

"Wait and see," my grandmother commanded. "But the chief is going to learn that true authority and power doesn't come from a titled position. It comes from making a lot of friends."

My head went through the list of people Nana might have called upon, and my fear and doubt over losing dissipated. No one played against my grandmother and got out of the game without being a little roughed up.

David pushed his way to the front of the crowd and caught sight of me. "Her. Let us talk to her," he called out.

The crowd of fae pushed forward to see who the half-dryad wanted to speak to, and the wardens struggled to keep them back.

Disobeying the chief's orders, I stepped forward, careful to take notice of the two small bodies and give them a wide berth. "Chief," I yelled for him to hear me over the din. "Let me talk to him. I think I can help with the situation."

He gazed at me, struggling to decide if he should let me help. When the fae pushed back on the wardens' hold again, he gave in. "Fine. Make it quick."

David convinced his colleagues to quiet down. He waited for me in the no man's land with the two dead pixies. "I found them like that. We heard they were going to arrest your grandmother, and they wanted to talk to the warden to stop them," his voice trembled.

"I'm so sorry. Do you have any idea who might have done it?" I asked.

A few in the back screamed out accusations that a witch did it.

The sprite who spoke to me before pushed her way to the front. "Why would one of us want to kill our own? No, it has to be one of them." She pointed her toilet brush at the wardens.

A tiny spark erupted in the wardens' shield where she aimed. For whatever reason my grandmother was privy to, the fae's powers were not as dampened as the wardens expected. If the sprite or any of her compatriots figured that little tidbit out, everyone in the area would find out what we all knew in Honeysuckle—the fae had far more power than most suspected.

"David, we need to keep things calm," I pleaded with the half-dryad. "I have a feeling everything is going to work out soon enough. But if you and your friends do any damage, you'll create a bigger mess."

"We want to know that we will be taken seriously and that someone will find out who took Flit and Fleet's life. If the big man there will guarantee that, I will do my best to calm them down," David proposed. "Also, we want the pixies to be treated with respect."

"That I guarantee." I glanced over at the bodies. "I'm so sorry," I repeated.

"Me, too." David took a deep breath. Turning back to the group, he waved his hands in the air. They quieted enough to listen to what he had to say.

I closed the distance between me and the chief. "They

want you to treat the death of the pixies with respect and to promise you will do your best to discover who did it."

The man wrinkled his nose. "Those things think they can make demands?"

His words upset me enough that I considered crossing sides and joining David and his friends. "They are not *things*. They are fae. Each one has a different lineage and culture, and they deserve to be treated with respect. See what happens when you do?"

I gestured at his line of wardens who no longer struggled to keep up a shield. The hotel workers on the other side stood quietly, watching me talk and waiting for the chief's answer.

The man in charge considered his options. "What was it they wanted again?"

"They want to be heard. They want the dead pixies to be treated the same way you would if they were witches." I listed out the few demands David gave me. "You can do that or you could see how long your wardens will last. You wanted others to see you in charge? Now's a perfect time to make the right choice."

He hesitated, and a murmur of unrest rippled through the group of fae. Taking a deep breath, he called out his order. "All wardens, stand down."

Looking at each other, his deputies dropped their hands and the shield disappeared.

"You and you and you, stay here and take statements from anyone willing to talk. Jones, I want you to guard the bodies until I call in more help." The chief shot me a side glance of irritation. "I will deal with these two."

As the wardens scrambled to carry out his new orders, the lights flashed on and off. The noise of the hotel ground to a halt, and we were plunged into silent darkness.

"What in fresh Hades is going on now?" the chief barked.

The lights returned after a tense minute, and I watched a big grin spread on Nana's face. She winked at me, and I prepared myself for something amazing to happen.

A light purple glow appeared in mid-air in the space between the chief and David. It extended down until it opened, ripping a hole in the room.

A bright floral scent wafted in the air, and a lilting voice I recognized breezed through. "*Aspetta, signore.*"

Chapter Nineteen

Agent Giacinta fluttered through the ripped entrance from the fairy path. *"Mi displace del ritardo,"* she addressed me. "I wish we might meet under better circumstances in the future."

"Who are you and how did you get in here?" Chief Huxley blinked and examined the sparkling portal until the space knitted itself closed and disappeared.

The fairy's presence both reassured me and provided evidence to back up my suspicions of my grandmother working something behind the scenes the entire time we'd been here. No doubt, Giacinta's arrival tied into the incremental increase of power from the fae.

The tiny agent's wings flapped as she hovered by me, lavender dust floating down onto the floor. She approached the crowd of fae watching her with cautious gazes, ignoring the wardens all together. "My friends, you will no longer have your freedoms hindered. I ask for your patience as my agents and I sort through the travesty that has ruled your lives for far too long."

Large tears rolled down David's face. "How can you guarantee that?"

"Oh," the fairy agent tittered. "I didn't introduce myself, did I? I am Agent Giacinta of the International Magical Patrol, and for now, this situation and the magical community of the city are under my authority."

"But you're a fae like us," the surly gnome I'd encountered before piped up.

Giacinta's wings quivered. "I am, and after we are finished fixing things, any of you could have the opportunity to work with me or anywhere you choose. But for now, I ask for your patience and cooperation." She glanced down at the two bodies underneath her. "I will have my colleagues come down here to investigate."

The chief stepped forward. "I've already assigned some of my force to handle interviews."

Finally acknowledging his presence, the fairy agent bobbed in front of him. "Good. Then they can assist my agents. You will be needed upstairs."

"I still don't understand how you got in here or who you think you are, taking over like this," Chief Huxley huffed.

"If you don't agree with the IMP agent in charge, then you can accept my authority, Chief." Deputy Inspector Pine from the World Organization of Wardens joined us.

The chief relaxed a bit. "Finally, a friendly face. What in the Sam Hill is going on?"

The deputy inspector raised his eyebrows. "I think it best, Chief Huxley, if you would comply with whatever orders the agent gave you." His eyes widened as if to convey some unspoken message. "Understand?"

The chief screwed up his face. "If you say so, Pine."

"All will be explained in short order." Agent Giacinta greeted others from her agency entering the room and gave them strict instructions.

David called me over to him. "Is she someone you trust?"

I nodded with enthusiasm. "I've worked with her before. She and her organization will make sure all of you will be able to live as you please. You'll be free to make your own choices for your lives."

He accepted my assurances, and I returned to the fairy and my grandmother.

"*Va bene,*" Agent Giacinta exclaimed. With a flourish, she produced her wand and waved it over Nana's ankle monitor, which unlocked and dropped onto the floor.

"Thank you, Agent," my grandmother gushed in relief.

"*Prego.*" The fairy got rid of her wand with another flick of her hand. "If you would please allow me to escort you upstairs, we may begin."

"Begin what?" I hated sounding as ignorant as the chief, who grumbled his way up the staircase.

Nana encouraged me to follow him but held me back at the last second. "To make the final play of the game."

I narrowed my eyes at her. "You've been working with them all along, haven't you?"

Without answering, she nudged me forward, and the three of us made our way to the ground floor. We walked down a deserted corridor to the hall where the food had been set up. The aroma of the leftovers caused my stomach to growl out loud.

The fairy directed the chief and my grandmother into the big hall but led me into a smaller room. She hovered at the door, and I addressed her before entering. "I have to say, I've never been so happy to see you, Agent Giacinta."

She grinned and winked. "Perhaps after we finish here, you would allow me the honor of taking a meal with you. And then maybe you will call me Gia. All my friends do."

It warmed me to have her call me her friend, but I knew better than to do so in front of the unhappy chief. When I entered the smaller room, my friends surrounded me, all of them trying to update me about what they'd heard or seen. I did my best to decipher all of the information but got lost in the tumult of excitement.

"Would y'all be quiet and move out of the way so I can get to my sister?" Matt pushed between Blythe and Lily, and I launched myself at him.

"What are you doing here?" I managed to choke out through my sudden tears.

My brother hugged me hard. "You think word gets out about our grandmother about to get arrested for murdering somebody and we don't all hear about it? I've been trying to get into the hotel now for hours. It took the arrival of WOW and IMP to get the local wardens to drop the wards."

"But we haven't been able to use our spell phones because of the wards. Except that one time. Did Nana call you?" I asked.

"Nana got word to us in Honeysuckle the night of the murder when she was taken to the station. She used her one phone call they allowed her to set things in motion." Matt explained. "Because of her connections, she's had a whole army fighting her battles on the outside."

"And all of us fighting for her on the inside." I gestured at my group of friends milling around and comparing notes.

"I think it's got to be the daughter," Lily claimed. "I heard that her relationship with her mother had deteriorated lately. And it was her name her mother called out before she died. Someone told me Peyton supposedly supported the group of witches who wanted to overthrow Priscilla."

"See, that's who I think orchestrated the death," her cousin Lavender countered. "There are two or three of the ladies who had good reasons to want the leadership to change."

"Would they kill to make that happen? Seems like an extreme way to alter things," I asserted. "Mason and I spoke to Frances, the woman who moderated the first panel. I know for sure she was in direct conflict with Priscilla, even though she claims she didn't kill her."

"Isn't that what all suspects say?" Blythe joked. "They all say they didn't do it, but someone has to be guilty."

"Just not Nana," I claimed. Looking around, I noticed a person missing. "Where's Mason?"

"He's talking to a WOW inspector, giving his impression of how the chief has mishandled everything from the beginning," Matt replied.

"And Ben's doing his advocate thing, making sure your grandmother is legally covered." Lily sighed loud and long. "I sure do love a smart man."

"We're hard to come by," my brother quipped.

I snorted and he elbowed me. The return to somewhat normalcy relieved a lot of my tension and my brain had room to think through all the possibilities for who took Priscilla's life. Even though the nasty woman had more people than most who wouldn't be sad at her funeral, she only had a select few who would truly benefit from her absence. And one daughter who inherited everything.

"So, is this where the party's happenin'?" John D escorted Mama Lee into the small space. We jostled around to give them room to enter and I introduced them to my friends.

I gave the older lady a hug. She leaned back and patted the spot on my chest where the mojo bag lay. "Good girl. I knew the root would work on you."

"I definitely feel luckier now than I did a few minutes ago. What are you doing here?" The lady's presence surprised me in more ways than one. For someone who kept out of Charleston witch society's business, she stood smack dab in the middle of the storm now.

"Your grandmother called me the night they took her into

the warden station." She held both my hands in hers. "We had been prepared for her to report something bad after attending the conference. What we didn't anticipate was anyone targeting her for a murder."

"Why do you think the wardens focused on Nana? Was it out of revenge for what happened with Calhoun Ravenel?" I'd been struggling to find a reason behind the unfair treatment of my grandmother the entire time.

"Cal got himself into trouble all on his own. Even his sister didn't think his approach against your town was smart," John D stated with a little disdain in his voice. "The chief has been in the pocket of a few of the older families in town for some time."

"They ain't gonna like the changes coming at 'em now, but they'll take their medicine if they know what's good for 'em." Mama Lee cackled hard.

Agent Giacinta hovered at the door. "*Mi scusi*. Oh, your group has grown in number, Charli." She nodded her head in admiration. "May I ask for you all to join me in the other room?"

We filed out and walked together into the room where the dinner had been served. All of the tables were folded and stacked against the walls. Several chairs were set up in a semi-circle with an aisle down the middle. A number of people sat in them, waiting, while Nana stood talking to a person in charge. Our group followed the fairy agent to the seats in the front two rows. Giacinta held me back and asked me to take the chair on the end.

I glanced over at Peyton sitting across from me. Although she remained my biggest suspect, she wore innocence like an old suit. Then again, murderers hardly ever looked like the mustache-twirling villain. Well, maybe only the chief did.

The fairy agent fluttered to the front and waited for the murmurs to die down. "All right. As you say in this country, we have our hands full at this moment."

"I would like to know why you have detained those of us who volunteered to come tonight," Peyton complained from her seat across from me. "We provided hospitality to those who have been stuck in this hotel and for that, we are rewarded by being held here?"

Agent Giacinta held up her hands. "If you would permit us some leeway, I am sure you will understand why those of you were chosen to stay. First, let me express my condolences to you for the loss of your mother."

Peyton thanked her with a nod, and the fairy agent continued while bobbing in the air. "We have begun to allow those not involved to check out of the hotel and return home while we discuss what has happened."

I sucked in a breath. "Oh, no. Abigail." Yes, I was mad at my cousin, but I had too many questions that needed answers.

"I'll go find her," Mason whispered to me. He excused himself and left before I had time to stop him or thank him.

Chief Huxley stood up. "I am still unclear as to how you can come into my town and think you can take over *my* authority."

"I would sit down and listen if I were you," Nana warned.

"Would you like to take over, Vivian?" Agent Giacinta asked, giving her the center stage spot.

"Gladly. There are several loose ends that need tying up and some explanations given." My grandmother's eyes flashed to mine. "Ever since the Charleston district made noises about wanting to take over Honeysuckle, I put my feelers out to find out more about your magical community here. And what I discovered disturbed me to no end."

"What we do here is none of your concern," the chief spit out.

"And yet, someone on your witches' council decided what we did was yours. Turnabout, Chief, is fair play," Nana challenged. "I didn't understand how underhanded your witch community had been all these years or I would have acted sooner."

"It's not your fault, Vivi," Mama Lee called out from her seat behind me. "We all weren't aware of how deep the treachery went. Every one of you who lives here should be ashamed of how you've treated folk who are different from you. But that's all changin' now."

"What did you and your voodoo do now, Letitia?" Chief Huxley asked.

John D stood so he could look at the chief directly. "It's Hoodoo, sir, and if you aren't willing to show us some respect, then I suggest you listen to the kinder lady up front and stay quiet until she finishes."

"What she did, Chief, is help me take down the magical enchantment, spells, and wards that controlled the magic of the fae here. As of now, all of the non-witch magical beings that have been living here have their full capacity of magic back," my grandmother explained.

"And the beautiful wrought iron fences and designs all over the area have been returned to their decorative purposes instead of being used to broadcast the corrupted magic that oppressed them in the first place," finished Mama Lee.

Peyton rose from her seat with slow deliberation. "I have been aware of the unfair treatment of other magical beings all of my life. Mother revealed the secret to me about the spell that kept them subjugated when I came of age. I had been trying to figure out a way to break the magic for some time now, as have a few others." She turned around to give credit to some of the witches sitting behind her. "If you have found a way to abolish the draconian enchantments, then you have my deepest gratitude."

Pretty words from a pretty girl. Either she was the greatest actor in the world, or my gut instincts were pushing me in the wrong direction.

"It took great effort from several different sides." Nana nodded acknowledgment to Mama Lee and John D as well as the nearby agents of IMP and inspectors from WOW. "And now, those of you who live here will have to learn how to incorporate any magical being who chooses to stay as equals. The days of 'witches only' are over."

Loud high-pitched cheers and claps erupted from the back of the room. Agent Giacinta gestured for the hotel staff to join the rest of us. David took Mason's vacated seat and

Blythe moved down to allow Molly to sit next to him. With a little rearranging, the fae staff sat amongst us, not in the back of the crowd.

Even while under house arrest, Nana managed to help take down corruption. Admiration and love for my grandmother swelled in my chest until I thought my heart might burst. If I could ever end up being half the witch she was, I'd consider myself lucky.

"Right, now that we've established what's happening on a bigger scale, we still have Priscilla's death to solve." Nana turned to face me. "The floor is all yours, Charli."

Chapter Twenty

My stomach dropped when everyone's attention turned to me. My grandmother gestured for me to stand up. With reluctance, I pushed out of my chair and approached her.

"I don't know what in tarnation kind of operation you're allowing to go on, Agent," the chief spit out, his mustache twitching at the ends from his frown. "But I, for one, have no intention of giving any credence to what this young woman has to say. She's not in law enforcement and she's kin to one of the suspects."

While his outburst broke the focus on me, Agent Giacinta addressed the angry chief, and I pulled Nana aside. "What are you doing? This is your show, not mine."

My grandmother stroked the back of her fingers down my arm with affection. "I may have been working things on the outside, but I never for a second doubted your skills in working the investigation from the inside. In fact, I counted on it."

"But I didn't do it alone." I glanced back at my friends.

I saw the seat David now occupied, wishing I had Mason there for back up instead. Lee, Alison Kate, Lily, and Lavender sat forward in their seats, waiting for me to speak. Blythe gave me two thumbs up and mouthed, "You can do it."

Nana reached down and took my hand in hers. "No, you weren't alone. But you figured out how to utilize everyone to the best of their abilities, and I would bet you have an idea who did everything if you calmed down and believed in yourself the way I do. You don't need your unique magical talents to be special, Charli. You already are just by being you."

I raised my eyebrow. "Okay, now you're laying it on a bit thick."

"But it's true, Birdy. Now, go get 'em." She squeezed my hand three times and let me go.

Agent Giacinta floated close to the chief to keep him in line. I surveyed all the faces staring back at me until my eyes rested on Peyton.

A strange calm settled inside me, and I took a deep breath. "What strikes me as odd with this particular murder is that, for the most part, not one person has truly mourned over Priscilla Ravenel Legare's passing. That speaks volumes about who she was to many people."

Peyton fidgeted in her seat, and I kept her in my peripheral vision to observe her reactions to my statements.

"While asking around to get a bit more context about who she was," I continued, "one person told me it would be easier to come up with a list of people who didn't want her gone."

Murmurs rippled through my small audience. A few of the local witches whispered to each other behind their hands. Not one person denied the statement.

I paced at the front. "Now, some of my history about Priscilla is unclear. For example, I don't know how long she has dominated the Charleston witch community nor do I know when she started terrorizing it."

Meg, who sat next to Peyton, glared at me with anger burning in her eyes. She clung to the daughter's arm with a firm grip while Peyton hid her eyes with her hand.

Moving down the aisle with slow steps, I stood at the side of a few Charleston witches. "But I do know that some of you had gotten to your end point. You wanted her gone from her dominant position over you. And therefore, you plotted to take her out."

The one sitting next to Frances sprung out of her seat. "We were trying to help the magical community at large. All we wanted was to change how things worked in our city. We were tired of having to do everything she asked, and we did have a plan to make her step down. But none of us are killers. We wouldn't do that to Peyton." She collapsed into her chair and raised a hanky to her face to wipe away the tears rimming her eyes.

Her friends comforted her and shouted their own protests to killing Priscilla. I held up my hand to stop them. "I think you had strong motives to want her removed from her position, but I agree. You didn't have any reason to want to end her life. Although there was someone who recently had a fight with Priscilla and may have wanted to take care of the problem before Priscilla could take care of them first." I took a step sideways to bring Frances into view.

With a stoic expression, the witch stood to face scrutiny. She matched my gaze. "You're right. Context does give a better understanding of things."

Since she understood who I was and who I was related to, I could finally push her to reveal more. "In your altercation with Priscilla at the Hyperion Hall a couple of months ago, what was the cause of your fighting?"

With nowhere to go and too many people surrounding her, Frances didn't protest or avoid answering. "Prissy knew who I sided with and had decided I would be the weakest link in the group to betray them and tell her everything they'd planned to force her out of her position months before that. She threatened to blackball me, not just from our magical community here, but all up and down the Southeast coast. Charleston is my home. My family's home. I couldn't leave. So, I played the subservient victim and did anything she asked until I couldn't take it anymore."

"What happened that particular night at the hotel hall?" I pushed.

"I tried to use her own tactics against her. I told Prissy

that if she didn't stop and step down, then I would reveal the dirty secret she would never want others to know. At first, she didn't believe I knew anything, but as I spilled all of the details to her, she blanched, and for a split second, I thought I'd won." Frances' eyes flitted to Peyton sitting a couple of rows in front of her. "I've never been sorrier about revealing what I knew for my own advantage. It brought more suffering than it needed to, and Prissy didn't fall for it. She called my bluff, knowing I couldn't actually go through with the telling of it all. So, I remained her favorite witch to punish."

"And all that punishment went away when she was killed," I concluded. "Your problems disappeared the second Priscilla took her last breath."

Frances wrung her hands in front of her. "I don't deny that. But I do deny having anything to do with her death. I was nowhere near her that entire night."

"But did her death require the killer to be near her? To know that, we'd have to know the examiner's findings. Chief Huxley," I walked to the front of the audience. "What was the cause of death?"

The head warden crossed his arms and slumped down in his chair. "I don't have to tell you anything."

Agent Giacinta snapped her tiny fingers, and one of her agents wearing a suit stepped forward with a file in his hand. "It states on the coroner's report that the victim died from a constriction of the airway, causing a blockage of oxygen. Death from suffocation."

"And does it state anywhere in the report what might have been the cause of the constricted airway?" I asked.

He flipped through the pages a couple of times. "No. There's a note here that says, 'Poison,' with a question mark but no further findings."

"No tests were run on the body? No toxicology examinations of her blood to determine the cause?" I pressed, anticipating his answer in the negative.

Suspecting someone had hindered justice and knowing it were two different things. With unspoken permission from Agent Giacinta, I towered over the chief where he sat. "Is it possible there was no discovery as to the cause of death because someone in a high position had the murderer all picked out. No need to find real evidence if the suspect is handed to them on a platter."

Chief Huxley sat up. "Hey, I'm not the one on trial here."

"If you were, we all know what your verdict would be," I challenged. "Is there anything you would like to add that might enlighten us as to why you wouldn't want to find the actual killer?"

The chief threw his chair back and faced me. "Hey, I had every reason to detain your grandmother. Witnesses heard her threatening words earlier and she was seen pursuing Priscilla and her daughter to the second floor. No other evidence was found to conclude she wasn't the murderer."

I pointed to the floor beneath us. "There are two witnesses downstairs who never had a chance to give their testimony. David, what did they tell us when you and I met on the roof?"

The half-dryad pushed his hair out of his face. "Fleet saw her," he pointed at Nana, "not entering the upper level of the hall. Instead, she went to the bathroom. The pixie and her brother Flit witnessed the mother and daughter fighting in the grand ballroom. But not her. Someone might have known that from the beginning if anybody paid us fae any attention." He slouched lower in his seat, and I appreciated Blythe offering him immediate comfort for his efforts.

"Nana, why had you followed Priscilla and Peyton in the first place?" I had yet to ask her the reasons behind the actions that got her into trouble to begin with.

"Peyton had been kind enough to push her mother into offering me an apology for her behavior during the first panel," my grandmother explained. "Priscilla all but apologized, which didn't make me happy. When I saw Peyton follow her mother upstairs, I thought I could address my issues with Priscilla and bury the proverbial hatchet once and for all. And I recognized family strife when I saw it. I thought maybe I could save the daughter from a fight with her mother if I were present."

"And why didn't you interfere once you were there?" I followed up.

Nana sighed. "Family business is just that. Their business. In the end, I didn't think me sticking my nose in would help Peyton at all. And I realized how futile it would be to try and force Priscilla to be nicer." She glanced at Peyton. "I will always wonder what I might have prevented had I stepped in despite my instincts."

"And without the testimony of the pixies, it was just your word that you weren't there in the same room or with Priscilla moments prior to her death." I finally addressed the one who met every single criteria. "Which leaves us with one person who had direct access to the victim. And out of anybody else here, the one who gained the most by her death."

Peyton popped up so hard, her chair fell over with a thud. "I didn't want my mother dead. I just wanted her to stop being so rigid about her rules and to bring an end to how she ran things."

Meg rose to join her at her side. "You did nothing wrong, pet." She rubbed Peyton's back.

"No, can't you see? Mother's behavior caused all of this to happen. If she would have been more like you, kind and caring, wanting to help others instead of using fear to rule over them, then she wouldn't have had so many people who went against her. Myself included."

Agent Giacinta winged her way closer. "Then are you offering a confession?"

Peyton's entire body began trembling. "I-I think I did want her gone. Deep down. I might have even said it out loud a few times. But I could never...I would never...But if I didn't do it, then who would have?"

"Shh, don't you worry." Meg stroked Peyton's hand. "I've always promised you everything would be okay. A girl as pretty as you deserves a beautiful world full of possibilities, not gates and cages."

Peyton covered her mouth with her other hand, a tiny cry squeaking out of her. "No," she whispered. "Tell me you didn't."

Like a rush, the whole puzzle came together. I had thought I was better than the witches in Charleston who ignored the fae and other magical beings who were thought of as being lesser. But I had fallen into the same pattern, completely ignoring one more being who would benefit the most from Priscilla's death. Or rather, the one who would kill to give the daughter-of-her-heart the life she thought she deserved.

"Meg," I uttered, surprised and resolved at the same time.

Peyton waved her hands. "No, no. It was me. I did it. I confess." Her lips quivered, and she stepped in front of the brownie. "Take me. I'm the one who killed my mother."

Chapter Twenty-One

❧❦❧

M eg gently pulled on Peyton. "It's okay, child. Everything will be okay."

The distraught young woman crouched down so she could address the brownie at her eye level. "Why?"

Running her gnarled fingers through Peyton's hair to push it away from the pretty girl's face, Meg's lips spread in a peaceful smile. "Because I couldn't let her try to shame you and keep you from living the life you want. Now you can love whomever you choose without any consequences."

Peyton broke into uncontrolled sobs, and she fell to her knees, burying her head into the brownie's body. Meg patted her on her back and whispered soothing words to the broken girl.

"*Mi dispiace*, but we will need your full confession," Agent Giacinta interrupted, regarding the scene with remorse.

"I know," uttered the brownie, consoling Peyton until she quieted her. "For the record, the only regret I have is not having the courage to do what I did sooner. And I'm real sorry about your involvement, Ms. Goodwin."

I recalled her telling me to untangle the web from before. I hadn't expected her to be the spider in the middle of it.

"Why would you kill her at all? If she was a terrible boss, then you could have left like your sister did. Why stay if Priscilla was worthy of being murdered?" I asked.

Meg helped Peyton sit back down in her chair. Once her charge was safe and secured, the brownie addressed the rest of us. "I stayed because of my love for Peyton. When this child was born, I thought maybe her presence would soften Priscilla. Help her to want to make the world better for her own offspring. Instead, it increased her desire to gain more control. She saw Peyton as an asset for her to use, not as a daughter to care for. So, I loved her doubly as much to try and make up for her mother's shortcomings."

A soft whimper from Peyton interrupted her. Meg moved to stand beside her, petting her head while she continued. "Priscilla did her best to break Peyton's spirit. She never let her go very far away, even forcing her to attend the college right here in Charleston despite my girl getting a full scholarship into the state university in Columbia."

Peyton sniffed and tried to pull herself together. "I wouldn't have even applied if it hadn't been for you pushing me. And my life would have been far grayer if you hadn't made sure the sun shone on me once in a while." Fueled by sudden desperation, the young woman stood in defiance. "You can't arrest her. You just can't."

Nana spoke first. "I'm sorry, Peyton."

Agent Giacinta moved in closer and beckoned her agents to follow. "We will have to accept your nanny's confession."

Peyton placed her arms around Meg's shoulders. "She isn't my nanny. She's...she's my family. She's all I have left in the world." Tears streamed down her face. "This is all my fault. Mother and I had a falling out when she found out I was seeing a guy from Beaufort who was half-brownie. He reminded me so much of you, my sweet Meg."

For the first time, the brownie's calm demeanor broke. "Thank you, pet. But I fear your choice angered your mother even more. It was as if you were choosing me over her, and she would never let you get away with that. She would have terrorized and bullied you until she'd broken you, and I couldn't live with myself if I allowed that to happen. I couldn't stand by and watch her reshape you into a mirror image of herself. I couldn't let you become your mother."

Peyton took her turn to console the brownie. She cupped Meg's chin in her hand. "She was never my real mother."

The brownie broke down and snatched Peyton in her arms, gathering her in an embrace. The two of them held on tight to each other until they had no more tears to cry.

Sniffles and utterances of pity spread throughout the room. I shuffled over to Nana, losing the battle to hide my own emotions. "Isn't there something we can do?" I whispered.

"I don't think so. Even if she committed the crime for noble reasons, she still killed somebody," Nana admitted. "Life sometimes isn't fair."

Meg gathered her wits about her and pushed Peyton away from her. "What have I always told you?"

Peyton dabbed her finger under her eye to catch a stray tear. "To live my life to its fullest and to the benefit of others."

I reached out to touch my grandmother, no longer able to hold back my own heartbreak. Hearing similar words of wisdom and love being exchanged made me regret my ability to solve the mystery at all.

A door in the back of the room slammed open. "My sister didn't do it. I did."

Wiping the tears from my eyes with the back of my hand, I watched Molly cross the span of the room on her short legs. The other brownie slowed to a stop as she stood next to Meg and Peyton.

"*Non ho capito*. Now there are two confessions?" questioned Agent Giacinta.

Molly stood with her arms crossed. "No. Only mine. I did it. I killed Priscilla, and that's the final word. You can arrest me and take me away, but my sister stays."

Nana and I exchanged glances, unsure of what to do and glad we didn't have to make the final decision. "If you committed the murder, then tell us how you did it," I insisted.

"While Priscilla and Peyton were arguing in the ballroom

upstairs, I brought them both glasses of champagne. I had slipped a lethal dose of belladonna into the one Priscilla took." Molly hardly blinked as she explained the act that killed a person.

I conferred with Nana. "Does that match Priscilla's death?"

"Belladonna," my grandmother repeated. "Also called Deadly Nightshade. In small doses, it can be medicinal, but it doesn't take much to kill a person. And it can burn the throat, cause hallucinations, flushed skin, and can constrict airways. Yes, it's definitely possible that's how Priscilla died."

"It's how it was done," Molly insisted. "I killed her because of her horrible treatment of people like me and her hold on my sister."

"I didn't stay because of the mother," Meg protested, unhappy at the turn of events.

The left side of Molly's lips curled up in a sad grin. "I know that now." She cleared her throat. "So, you'll be arresting me and not my sister."

Agent Giacinta flapped her wings in agitation. "This is most irregular. I have ways of forcing the truth, but I am torn as to what to do in this situation."

Chief Huxley snorted. "I say arrest them both. Throw their tiny behinds in jail where they can rot for the rest of their lives."

"Which is why you have been relieved of your position, sir," the fairy agent retorted. "If you refuse to do your job to the letter, then you force others to step in until a suitable replacement can be found. But for the moment, I wish to confer with Deputy Inspector Pine."

She sent an agent to retrieve him from handling the deaths of the two pixies on the floor below us. While we waited, Nana held the chief in her intimidating glare.

"What? What do you want?" he grunted.

"I think you have something that doesn't belong to you." My grandmother pointed at his pocket.

He rummaged around and pulled out the item. "Oh, yeah." The chief held the ring up, the emerald flashing bright green.

"The Ravenel ring!" Peyton exclaimed. "Where did you find it?"

Nana looked to Agent Giacinta as she threw out her accusation. "I believe the chief planted it in my room for me to find so that he could use it to justify arresting me."

"I did not put it in your room," the corrupt head warden claimed. "I did, however, respond to a call that suggested we search you for the ring."

Nana's eyebrows raised high on her forehead. "And that didn't sound suspicious? Like somebody was trying to set me up? Or did you just accept it because it fit your plan."

He sneered. "Doesn't matter now, does it?"

Deputy Inspector Pine arrived, surveying all of us with subjective scrutiny. "What have I missed?"

"They think they have the authority to remove me from my position. Tell this fairy she can't do that, Pine," the chief demanded.

"I can't do that, Huxley." The deputy inspector shook his head and pursed his lips, sending an unspoken message that quieted the chief. He turned to listen to Agent Giacinta, getting caught up on the two confessions.

"Is it me, or does the WOW inspector seem a bit too friendly with the corrupt chief?" I asked Nana.

"That might be something to remember to check out later," my grandmother agreed. "For now, I think they're coming up with a decision."

We watched the two brownie sisters hug each other. Molly whispered something in Meg's ear that made the shorter one crumple into her. The two comforted each other and waited to be told the decision.

Agent Giacinta addressed the two. "I would like to state for the record that I do not believe that the differing confessions were given in order to confound or obstruct justice. I would ask both of you to confirm that you are offering to accept your culpability in the murder of Priscilla Ravenel Legare."

"I do confess as her killer," stated Molly.

"And you?" The fairy agent turned her attention to the shorter of the brownies. "Do you confess to the murder as well?"

"I do not," Meg protested. "I wish to clarify my false confession."

Gasps and murmurs of surprise echoed throughout the room. I watched Molly as her sister changed her story.

Meg held onto Peyton with one hand and her sister with

the other. "I wrongfully confessed because I suspected this beloved child to have committed the crime. I know it was wrong, but I couldn't bear for her to be taken away and found guilty of killing her mother when I could have saved her all along. I am sorry to find that my sister was the one to poison Priscilla, but I cannot lie any longer."

Meg's eyes darted to check with her sister, and I observed a shared intimate silent message sent between the two. Molly squeezed her sister's hand and let go. "There you have it. I'm the killer and Meg here stays with Peyton. That's the end of it."

Agent Giacinta sighed. "Then I believe we have a resolution to the murder, although I do not feel as if justice is truly being served." She directed her agents to collect Molly but held them back to allow the sisters to say goodbye to each other.

"Why do I get the feeling that the wrong person is going to be arrested?" I spoke out loud.

"I can't blame the poor brownie. Sometimes, we'll go to great lengths for our family. There isn't much I wouldn't do to protect you or your brother." Nana bumped my arm with hers. "And I know how much you've done for me here. Thank you, Birdy."

I caught the chief trying to sneak out while the agents were distracted. "We're not done quite yet," I said, pointing him out to the fairy.

An agent blocked the chief's path to freedom, and he

shambled back to his seat, refusing to sit down and staring at me.

"What do you mean?" Nana asked. "We've managed to break the spell that oppressed a considerable population of fae in this city and solved a murder. What else is left?"

Mason entered the room, dragging Abigail with him. My cousin caught sight of me and tried to run, but the detective held onto her tighter. Bringing her closer to us, he insisted she sit down in a chair behind my friends.

"If the chief didn't plant the ring, then who did?" I asked, glaring at my cousin.

The conundrum I faced frustrated me. I both wanted to know Abigail's involvement and didn't at the same time. But my instincts told me I couldn't leave parts of the web tangled and be satisfied. Even if it changed everything, I needed to know the truth about my family by blood.

Chapter Twenty-Two

A fter the agents cleared out most of the room, I beckoned Mason to bring Abigail forward to join me.

My cousin held up her hands. "Charli, I swear—"

"Don't," I stopped her. "The only thing I want to hear out of you right now is answers. Did you plant the ring in my grandmother's room?"

She shook her head. "No. That wasn't me. I really did want to help you find the ring, but when I realized where it must be, I couldn't go through with it."

"With what? Helping me? Or something else?" I pushed.

Abigail's face fell. "Please don't ask me any more questions."

Nana walked over to her. "I've been more than patient with you. Didn't address the fact that I couldn't find any records of an Abigail Wilson anywhere, which tells me either you appeared out of thin air or you're lying. Based on your behavior, I'm choosing the latter."

Matt stepped up to join her, blocking my view of my supposed cousin. "Are you even related? Or was that lie supposed to get you close to Charli?"

"I swear, we're related. I knew it the second I saw her," she called out.

I placed my hands on my brother and grandmother and moved them out of the way. "I saw it, too. But maybe I imagined we looked a little alike. When did you first become aware of me?"

Abigail stood a little straighter. "That part I told you about. Our family got word about someone with tracking powers using them and solving mysteries in your town. I can't say a whole lot, but my first time seeing you was during the weekend of the barbecue event. I was too scared to talk to you in person, so I left you the note instead."

"Why can't you say more?" Nana pushed. "What's stopping you?"

"Is it your parents? Siblings? I've been thinking about the few times you've slipped up, Abigail, and there's something you're not saying about our family," I accused. "What is it about them that has you so scared?"

Her eyes darted about her, and she shrunk into herself. "Please. If I fail them even more, you have no idea the consequences I'll face."

Matt took pity on her. "If you do tell us, maybe we'll be

able to help. But if you keep lying to us, then there's nothing we can do for you."

"Who were you talking to in your room? I know I heard a male voice coming from inside, and you tried to cover that up. Who was it?" I insisted.

Abigail gasped. "If I tell you, he'll tell Grandmama."

"Well, this grandmother may make sure you don't ever make it out of this town if you don't answer Charli's question," Nana threatened. When she got to the point where she played dirty, I knew trouble had arrived with a capital *T*.

"Since phones weren't working during the time we were here, I used the mirror to communicate with a family representative," Abigail explained. "He told me I had failed to collect evidence and that he would be employing his back-up plan."

"You mean, the ring? If you were trying to find it, too, then why did you stop using your magic with me?" My frustration grew with her cryptic answers.

"No. The use of the ring had two purposes. One, seeing what putting your grandmother under deeper threat would do to you and your magic. And two, using the quest for the ring to test your abilities." My cousin swayed on her feet, overwhelmed by the truth. "I never wanted to hurt you, Charli. Not after I got to know you. But you can't refuse the family."

"You keep saying that word as if it's a weapon or something being held against you," Matt observed. "Or as if it's some sort of illegal organization."

Abigail scoffed. "They hire many people to make sure whatever they do is never found illegal." Realizing she'd said too much, she threw her hand over her mouth.

I kept thinking back to the night of the murder. Although it had just happened, it seemed so long ago after all we'd gone through. "I remember that night you saw something that surprised you."

"I've never seen a person die before," she admitted.

"No, I know what shock over death looks like. That wasn't it. You recognized someone you didn't expect to see. Who else was there?" I tried to picture everyone on the balcony.

"A family representative." Abigail ran her hand down her face. "Oh, what's the use in protecting them any longer? When they come to fetch me, I'll be in trouble anyway. What you saw was my reaction to seeing my cousin Ethan as part of the crowd around the body. He's also who was talking to me through the mirror. He was supposed to be in the hotel with us, but he got locked out when they enacted the ward."

I tried picturing all of the men I'd seen that night and couldn't come up with an image. "Why was he here?"

"To observe my interaction with you and to make sure we tested your magic." Abigail spoke without restraint, a little manic from her decision to risk everything. "It's one thing to hear the stories. He was supposed to report back as to how strong you actually were. When I told him you no longer possessed your powers, I was actually glad you wouldn't be of use to them."

"What if I did get them back? Like when you and I

worked together. Did you tell Ethan my magic worked a little?" I tried not to scream in agitation.

When would my tracking powers ever stop being a minefield for me to navigate? Perhaps Abigail had the right idea. Not having them might be a better alternative than having to live with threats because I possessed the special talents.

My cousin shook her head. "I didn't tell him anything at all. As far as he or any of the rest of the family knows, you lost your abilities due to a misfired spell. As long as I stick to that story, you should be safe."

"For now," pushed Matt. "But will they be watching her the rest of her life?"

Her face fell again. "I don't know, but they won't send me again. I probably should say goodbye to you now because it's very unlikely we'll meet after today."

Anger, confusion, and longing mixed together until I didn't know which way was up. Pulling a chair closer to me, I plopped down into it. My friends tried to console me, but I pushed them all away. Nana spoke to them quietly while Matt kept a hand on my shoulder, allowing me to stew.

"I have a question," Nana raised her hand. "Who put the ring in my room if your cousin Ethan was locked out? There's another missing piece to the puzzle."

Abigail's brow furrowed. "I'm actually not sure who did it. It wasn't me and it wasn't him."

"I know who it was," David stated, joining us. He escorted

the very unhappy pink-haired half-fairy I'd met on the roof. "Rayna has something to tell you."

"No, I don't have anything to say to these witches." She spat on the floor.

David pushed her forward and pointed at her. "She's the one who put the ring in the room. And I think she killed Flit and Fleet."

My brother let go of my shoulder and adopted his warden authority in his voice. "Is this true?"

"I don't have to tell any of you anything. The money I was paid bought my silence," she crowed. "He promised if I got into trouble, I was to call him, and he would come."

"Was it Ethan who promised you that?" Abigail sneered. "Good luck getting him to follow through on a promise like that. Ethan looks out for Ethan."

"That's not true, cousin," a deep male voice called out from the back of the room. "Your words cut me to my core."

Ethan wore an impeccably tailored dark gray suit. He approached us while taking off the designer sunglasses he kept on while inside. When he stopped next to Abigail, she cringed away from him and he smiled with smug satisfaction at her reaction.

Reaching in his breast pocket, he pulled out a card. "Ethan Wilson, head advocate and legal advisor."

"See?" Rayna smirked. "I told you he would come to get me out of trouble."

The new cousin barely considered the half-fairy. "I'm

sorry, but I'm not sure I know who you are. Have we met before?"

Rayna's face dropped. "But you paid me to hide the ring. Gave me instructions on how to put it in the mirror."

Ethan considered the accusation. "No, I'm not sure what you're talking about. And if you were paid any money, I guarantee there would be no way to connect me or any of my family to it." He chewed on the end of his sunglasses. "And as for you killing two others, well, my office doesn't directly represent murderers."

"Ha!" The noise gushed out of Abigail, and she covered her mouth again.

Rayna panicked. "I only killed Flit and Fleet because they were going to ruin everything. You wanted that old woman there to be arrested. You told me so. If those two pixies talked to a warden, everything I've worked to gain would be over."

Agent Giacinta hovered closer after she'd returned to the room. She nodded at the agent with her, and he came to collect the half-fairy. Rayna's undersized wings flapped in frustration as she struggled to get away. Pity for another victim of the treatment of the fae in this city flashed for a moment until I remembered the lifeless bodies of the pixies. Needless deaths for needless reasons.

"As for you, cousin, I'm truly disappointed. Grandmama wants me to bring you to her ASAP. So, run along and get your things," Ethan commanded.

"Which cousin?" I challenged. "It seems to me if you're a

cousin of Abigail's, then you and I must be related as well." I stuck my hand out to shake his.

He eyed it with a bit of disgust. "No, I don't believe we will be claiming you after all. Everyone in my family has a particular talent that we share. According to Abigail, the rumors surrounding your so-called abilities were just that. Rumors."

I clenched my fingers into a fist, wondering how many bones I would break if I punched him in the face. Then again, I wouldn't want to leave that as my final impression for *the family*.

"Well, in my family, we don't require anything of anybody except to care for and look out for one another," I stated.

"And where has that gotten you? Stuck in a small Southern town with very little to your name whereas I am part of one of the richest witch dynasties," Ethan boasted, taking out his handkerchief to clean a spot on his sunglasses. "Too bad you're not going to be a part of it."

"My family is mine even though I don't share their DNA. In fact, I consider myself pretty rich in comparison. After all, I get to choose my family." I glanced around at my grandmother, my brother, and my friends. "A family made from love is stronger than blood anytime. That's something you can choose to learn, Abs."

My cousin perked up at my nickname for her, but Ethan snapped his fingers. "Abs. How quaint. Well, *Abs* will be bound by her promises to us and will return to the fold as she is told to do."

"I'd like to see you try and enforce that if she doesn't want to go back with you." I crossed my arms and stood toe to toe with Ethan, craning my neck to gaze up at his tall stature.

He sighed and placed his sunglasses back on. "I can assure you, my family is bigger and more powerful than yours."

"Don't bet on it." Nana held out both her hands in front of her and Matt stood on my other side. "I think we outnumber you at the moment."

"Three against one is not that many," Ethan scoffed.

"No," Mason said. "But Charli's got a much bigger family than you anticipated. Look around you."

All of my friends stood in solidarity with me, including David and Agent Giacinta. We couldn't see his eyes behind his glasses, but I watched his Adam's apple bob with a hard swallow when he counted our numbers.

Abigail approached me. "I should go with him."

After all of my bluster, she wanted to give in. "You don't have to. We can help you. I promise." The thought of losing contact with her erased my anger.

"I believe you." She touched my arm. "But if I voluntarily go back with him now, I think I can convince our grandmother that your powers are gone. Make sure they close their files on you."

Realizing she was willing to face whatever fed her fear about the family on my behalf, I wanted to beg her to stay and ask my grandmother to find a way to fix things.

Abigail grinned. "Don't bother arguing. I can be stubborn, too." She winked. "I learned that trait best from my cousin."

I threw my arms around her and hugged her tight. "Will you stay in touch?"

"Imph trmph" she muffled into my shoulder. I eased my hold on her and she spoke again. "I'll try."

"Don't just try," I insisted. "And when you're ready, you come find me again."

I let her go with reluctance. Ethan smirked and jerked his head for Abigail to leave with him.

"I will find a way to keep up with her. As you can see, I've got friends in lots of places." I indicated at the agents still in the room. "If I hear that she's been harmed in anyway, I assure you there will be consequences."

Ethan turned on his heel and walked away. "I will be sure to pass that along. Good luck with your chosen family. Come along, Abigail."

"I don't need luck," I bellowed at him. "I've got love on my side."

My cousin offered me a sheepish wave and hurried off. Watching her walk away with that villain broke something in me. I clutched my stomach, a queasy unsettled sensation overwhelming me.

"Are you okay, Birdy?" Nana asked, holding me up by my middle.

"No," I uttered, my voice empty and lifeless.

"But you will be." She kissed the top of my head, sealing her promise.

Chapter Twenty-Three

The hotel insisted we leave instead of staying one more night. None of us could blame them since my grandmother had been a catalyst for the immediate changes in its fae work force.

David offered to stay to assist with the transition and to help others like him understand their choices. Nana and Mason assured him that when he was ready, one of them would travel down to pick him up and bring him to Honeysuckle.

Peyton and Meg left together as one unit. I knew they both had a lot of healing to do, but they had each other to lean on. Through their struggle and the outcome of their circumstances, I understood far too well the importance of family.

All of my friends left on the bus headed back home. Since

Matt had driven his car to Charleston, Nana thought it best I travel home that way instead of the bus. Everyone spoke about me but nobody dared to speak to me. A desolate silence held my fragile sanity together by a thread.

Mason escorted me to the car and tucked me into the backseat. The detective allowed me a slight bubble of space but continued to be there for me. I would have protested that I didn't need him, but any words I could form to say so wouldn't have been true.

Leaning my head against the window, I watched the afternoon sun highlight the beautiful historic houses that lined the Charleston streets. Intricate wrought iron artistry decorated the gates and fenced in secret gardens, and it saddened me to know how all of the iron work had been corrupted to oppress so many for so long. At least now, I could admire their beauty without guilt.

We drove over a bridge spanning across the water. A snowy white egret spread its wings and soared next to us. The orange glow of the last afternoon sunlight dappled through the trees as we drove down two-lane roads, and I closed my eyes to watch the dance of light and darkness against my lids.

I jerked awake when the car turned down a dirt road and bumped through a pothole. Matt slowly drove to a small parking lot next to a wooden cottage and pulled into an empty spot up front.

Nana got out of the front passenger seat and opened my car door. "Time to get out, Birdy."

"Where are we?" I asked, not budging.

"When you unbuckle your seatbelt and get out, you'll see." She tapped her foot on the ground. "Now or never."

I leaned back in my seat. "You go. I'll wait here."

Mason got out and walked around until he blocked my view of my grandmother. Leaning over, he unbuckled me.

"I'm not a child," I insisted, holding back my lower lip from pouting.

"I know. But your grandmother is going to get her way, so why fight it?" He offered me his hand to help me out.

Matt looked at me in his rearview mirror. "Come on, Birdy. I think you'll appreciate what Nana's set up for you. Plus, if you don't get out now, I'll make sure to find every pothole from here to Honeysuckle to make sure you can't sleep on the way home."

My brother rarely backed down from his threats. "Jerk," I mumbled.

"Brat."

My lips twitched up despite my mood. Trying to pull up my big witch panties, I accepted Mason's offer to help me out of the car. He held onto my hand for a brief extra moment, but I refused to meet his concerned gaze.

I pulled out of his grip. "I'm fine on my own."

"I know," he answered in a steady tone. "But we're all here in case you aren't."

A breeze rustled through the leaves of the trees and tickled the hanging Spanish moss, cooling our skin still warmed from the lingering heat and humidity of the day.

Voices carried in the air and my curiosity fueled my steps toward the sound.

"Wow." I stopped moving, too overwhelmed to do anything other than stand in awe.

A large live oak filled my view. Much like our Founders' tree, it stood in the middle of a clearing, its massive trunk making our native town tree seem like a sapling in comparison. Limbs grew out in twisted and gnarled arms, some of the thick branches dipping into the ground and back out. A few of the largest ones required braces to hold them up.

Matt stood next to me. "Wow is right," he exclaimed. "I'll never not be amazed when I see the Angel Oak."

When my brother spoke the name of the tree, a rush of memories flooded my mind. Mom and Dad had brought us to visit many years past. My brother and I had chased each other around, giggling and scrambling under and over the branches of the tree.

Nana passed us. "Stop dawdling, we've got work to do." Her demeanor broke the spell of amazement the tree cast on us.

More aware of my surroundings, I took stock of the group of people waiting for us under the canopy of the Angel Oak. I recognized only a few of the faces watching us, surprised to find some of the witches from Charleston who had wanted change standing behind Mama Lee, John D, Titia, and a bunch of people I didn't know.

The fairy agent left the side of the matriarch and flitted over to me. "This is very much like the tree in your town, no?"

"It is, Agent Giacinta," I confirmed. "They're both live oaks. They live a long time."

"Call me Gia, please." Her wings fluttered, scattering lavender dust into the air. "The energy here is palpable. The roots must tap into a natural line of power, much like your tree. I imagine generations of people and other beings have been drawn to it like we are now."

"Enough chit chat," demanded Nana. She gestured for me to join her next to Mama Lee.

The older woman beckoned me into her arms. She kissed my cheek and hugged me close. "Oh, child, I knew you had struggles comin'. But change doesn't happen without a few bruises." She pushed me away from her and checked me over like she had before. With a wink, she let me go. "You'll be fine soon enough. But you need one more push."

I didn't know how much more I could take and wanted to thank her and refuse at the same time. Nana placed her hands on my shoulders, holding me in place. She leaned in behind me, her breath tickling my ear. "Running away will only delay the pain, not end it. It's time to push through and fly, my little bird."

The sky glowed pink and orange with the oncoming setting of the sun. "We gonna run out of time," Mama Lee announced. "Let's form a circle around the tree."

"Not you, Birdy," Nana explained, guiding me to the large

trunk of the Angel Oak. She placed my hand on its rough bark. "You stay here, and no matter what, don't let go."

"Vivian, she needs someone to ground her," John D called out.

"I will," Matt declared.

Mason spoke at the same time. "I can do it."

"It's your choice, Birdy," my grandmother offered. "I need to stand with Letitia."

Mason had been a grounding force for me the whole time I thought Nana was in trouble. No, we weren't who we used to be, but something had been building between us even when we weren't paying attention. But whatever was happening right now, it felt too real and important.

"I want my brother," I declared, choosing the family member who'd always been there for me.

Matt joined us and took Nana's place beside me. He slipped his fingers through mine and curled them into a tight clasp.

Pointing at a branch, he chuckled. "Remember that photo of you, me, Mom, and Dad standing in front of this tree? I think we took it right over there."

The weathered picture must be in some album tucked away in a box in Nana's attic. I remembered us laughing a lot when it was taken. "Dad was leaning back on it with Mom holding me in her arms and you standing in front of both of them."

"And then Dad bought us ice cream bars to eat in the car," Matt mused. "He never let us eat in the car."

"But he did that day," I recalled. "Do you know what's going on right now?"

My brother shook his head. "But I trust Nana that this is important. If you get scared, just concentrate on being here with Mom and Dad. And I've always got you." He squeezed my hand three times, and I responded in kind.

Mama Lee raised her hands in the air. "Brothers and sisters, friends old and new, y'all are welcome here on this land. There was a time when all of us wouldn't have been able to share the same space, but today, we remember the past and gather together to build a better present and future. Through us, we will begin the healin'."

Standing between her great-granddaughter and her son, she closed her eyes and sang out a verse. Her kin answered her in song. They repeated the same pattern of performance, and I found myself entranced.

The sky darkened from pink to red above us, and I craned my neck to watch the last light filter through the canopy of the oak. The bark of the tree tingled beneath my skin and tendrils of power wove into me, holding me in place.

"Whatever happens, I've got you, Birdy," Matt promised.

Mama Lee and the circle surrounding the two of us focused their intent, and energy shot through me like an icy knife. Matt grunted, and the temporary pain disappeared for a moment until another flash of power hit me. Again and again, the magic ripped into me, and I gritted my teeth, holding back the screams, drawing strength from my brother. He acted as my lightning rod for the energy, absorbing the run-off and sending it back into the earth.

One final hit wrenched me wide open and energy poured into me like liquid into a glass pitcher until I could hold no more of it.

"Steady," Matt ordered.

"I can't. It's going to—" A shriek lifted in the air when the bomb of magic exploded out from my body. Someone snuffed out the sun, and darkness swallowed the world around me.

When I blinked my eyes open at last, cicadas sang their night tune and stars filled the sky. My stomach rumbled like distant thunder when I caught the scent of delicious food.

"She's awake," Matt declared. He thrust a glass into my hand. "Drink all this down."

The liquid cooled the embers of fire still warming my insides. I licked my lips. "That doesn't taste like normal sweet tea."

"It ain't." Mama Lee shuffled over and placed her hand on my forehead. "It's swamp water."

I spit out my next gulp, and she cackled.

The great-grandmother's namesake, Titia, rolled her eyes. "Stop messing with her, Granny. It's just a mix of lemonade and sweet tea, Charli."

"The sugar will help you recover faster, so stop expelling it and drink it all down." Nana's rough tone didn't hide her underlying concern for me.

"I'm fine," I assured everyone around me. Attempting to

stand, dizziness hit me and I sat back down. "Or I thought I was."

"Here, you can finish my glass and I'll get another." Mason took my empty one away and switched it with his.

Wanting to stop being the center of attention, I obeyed and replenished with more swamp water until I figured my bladder might burst. "What smells so good?" I asked.

Matt put his arm around my shoulder. "She must be feeling better if she's only concerned about eating."

Whatever had happened to me at the Angel Oak left me ravenous. My brother escorted me with care to the picnic tables and food set up in the night air.

No stranger to good food, my jaw dropped when I surveyed the many tables full of huge pots of steaming goodness. The generous bounty would give one of our many potlucks in Honeysuckle a run for its money.

Someone placed a plate in my hands, and I followed the line through the buffet of goodness. Before long, I'd loaded it up with fried chicken, fried okra, macaroni and cheese, collards with some of that delicious ox tail stew poured over them, and a tiny scoop of dirty rice. I had to skip the Lowcountry boil of shrimp, smoked sausage, corn, and red potatoes because of a serious lack of space.

During the conversation that flowed while we ate, I found out I'd been loaded back into the car and taken to Mosquito Beach, a part of the Sol Legare Preserve on James Island. The backyard belonged to Mama Lee, and she and her community had contributed to the food. I expected more people to be present, but only those whom I recognized surrounded me.

A little lavender dust floated onto my shrimp and grits, and Gia set a small plate of food next to me. "In my home country, we know how to cook, but I don't think I've ever seen people eat as much as you."

I scooped up a bite of stew and collards. "It helps feed our magic as much as our bodies," I explained. "Or at least that's my excuse."

The fairy agent pouted. "If I eat as much as you, I will gain a...*una pancia.*" She poked her belly. "It'll become hard for me to fly around."

"You could never be too fat to fly. Trust me, I know a certain cupid who manages it." She didn't need me to tell her how hard Skeeter had to work at it though.

It took a few trips to the buffet plus two helpings of sweet potato pie and a generous serving of bread pudding before I filled my giant hole of hunger. Mama Lee packed up leftovers in a cooler for us to take back with us.

"You sure you don't wanna stay the night?" she asked, walking us back to the car.

Nana hugged her goodbye. "I think we're all anxious to get back. My grandson will be fine to drive, and he's got help in case he gets tired. Thank you, Letitia."

"My dear friend, thank you for what you've done. Some of the wounds in our area may never fully heal, but through your efforts, a lot of good has come. At least some of the pain the troubles have caused may have a chance to be healed." The elder matriarch patted my grandmother on the back.

I opened my car door, but Mama Lee held me back. "Give me your mojo bag, child."

I slipped the leather cord off and handed her the requested object.

"You don't need it anymore, but you take this one home with you." She gave me a different one in exchange.

"What's this one for?" I asked, curious to know what she'd sealed into the soft cloth.

"A little of this and that." She watched Mason as he got into his side of the car. "Keep this close to you and watch what it brings into your life."

"That's all you're going to tell me? Not that it will bring me luck or fortune?" I couldn't say the other thing I suspected she wanted the mojo bag to bring me based on her admiration of the detective.

She stroked my cheek with her wrinkled hand. "What fun would life be without a few surprises? Take it easy for the next week or so. You've still got some leftovers from our tree's magic runnin' in you."

In my hunger, I hadn't thought about what had happened to me at the Angel Oak. Placing my hand over my chest, I searched to figure out if I felt different. "I will," I murmured.

"Move over, Mama, and let me hug this girl goodbye." John D enveloped me with his long arms. "When you get home, you put my painting up somewhere you can see it every day."

I gasped. "You're giving me one of your lithographs?"

"Nope, not a copy." He chucked me under my chin and winked. "I think seeing our tree will bring you joy and help you heal."

Titia waited her turn. "I hope you'll return sometime and let me share some real Lowcountry fun with you."

I didn't know when I'd have the courage to come back, but I promised her when I did, she'd be the first I'd call.

Gia zoomed over in a wake of purple dust and hugged me about my neck. "I hope the next time we see each other it will be for friendlier reasons. *Ciao, bella.*"

"*Ciao*, Gia." I did my best to imitate her accent and failed.

Once we got on the road, I settled into the backseat and closed my eyes.

"You okay, Charli?" Matt asked, checking on me in the rearview mirror.

We drove over a pothole and my left hand bounced until my pinky touched Mason's. He glanced at me, his eyes sparkling with care and a little mischief. His pinky hooked through mine and held on.

"I will be," I promised.

Epilogue

It took me more than a week to recover from Charleston and my visit to the Angel Oak. My friends and family insisted on visiting and feeding me at all hours of the day. The barn became the only place I could hide from their incessant attention since nobody believed me when I told them I was fine.

I fed another carrot to the baby unicorn, who I swear had grown bigger in the short time we were gone. It nuzzled my palm, searching for more goodies. The hair of its mane turned from pink to purple.

"That's a nifty trick you can do, sweetie," I crooned at the mythical creature. "But I don't have any more carrots for you."

The unicorn snorted a huff and offered me its head to rub instead. Careful of its horn, I scratched between her ears.

"I knew you'd be out here." Matt's voice echoed off the wooden walls of the barn. "If you're playing hide and seek, then you're not doing it right, standing out in the open like that."

"I'm not hiding, exactly. I just needed a little breathing room," I explained.

My brother wrinkled his nose. "And you wanted to breathe here?" He patted Rayline's back and bounced her in his arms.

"Don't talk to me about strange smells." I pointed a finger at my niece's bottom. "What comes out of there isn't exactly rose petals."

"Oh, I know. She blew out her diaper the other day." Matt closed his eyes at the memory. "It took me ages to clean everything up."

I took my niece from him and cradled her in my arms, trying hard not to shake her too much from my laughter. "Did you poo all over your daddy?" I held up her hand and gave her a tiny high-five. "Good job, Junior."

My brother opened his mouth and I could tell by his expression he wanted to ask if I was okay. I held up my hand to stop him.

"First, don't ask. Second, seriously, don't ask. Third, I'm really fine. And yes, it's truly awesome that my talents have been coming back. But no, I haven't heard from Abigail. Does that cover it all?" I challenged.

Matt regarded me for an extra moment before giving in. "Got it."

The unicorn whinnied and trotted over to visit the baby.

Rayline squirmed in my arms until I positioned her so she could sit up and see the funny pony. She reached out with her tiny digits and tried to squeeze around the unicorn's horn.

"Uh-uh, gentle, Sunshine." I pulled Rayline back so the baby wouldn't tug on the horn or strands of the mane that turned from purple to a bright green.

The unicorn neighed and leaned her head closer with slow deliberation, allowing the baby to touch her. Rayline squealed with delight and drooled.

"I think they might be each other's soul mates," I marveled.

Matt leaned on the pen. "I can't believe my daughter has a unicorn for a friend."

"We really should name her," I suggested. "Nobody should be nameless for too long, and if we wait for your daughter to be able to speak, the name might end up something dumb like Da-da."

"Hey," Matt complained, smacking my arm. "I can't wait for her to say Da-da."

Holding the baby prevented me from hitting him back, so I kicked him in the shin instead. "It'll get confusing if you and the unicorn are both Da-da."

"You've got a point," he conceded. "It should be something cute, like Dazzle or Twinkle or Bubbles."

I wrinkled my nose. "It won't be small forever. Maybe something more dignified like Opal or Pearl."

"She's not jewelry." Matt pondered more choices. "How

about something special like Splendor. Or Stardust. Or Glamory."

"Is that a word?"

"I don't know," he admitted. "But it sounds unique."

We came up with names based on food such as Pickles and Waffles and Ice Cream but dismissed those as too silly.

The unicorn backed away and shimmied for a second, its multi-colored tail lifting away from its body. With a nicker, she farted, and a cloud of rainbow sparkles sprayed out of her behind. Rayline giggled, and the creature neighed with happiness, trotting around her pen and returning for the baby to pet her again.

Matt stood with a dropped jaw. "If I hadn't seen it, I wouldn't believe it."

"Me neither." I nudged his mouth closed with my finger. "I think she just named herself."

"What? Rainbow Sparkles?" my brother asked.

Kissing the top of my niece's head, I breathed in that yummy baby scent. "If only you tooted like that, Junior."

"Oh, this little one does not produce rainbows. Trust me," Matt exclaimed.

The unicorn whinnied her approval and I stroked her ever-changing mane. "You like your name, Rainbow Sparkles?"

She shook her hair out and stomped on the floor of the stall.

"How about just Sparkles?" I asked.

The unicorn nodded its head, and I handed the baby back

to my brother to keep my niece from getting speared by the horn.

"Sparkles it is." Matt held Rayline up. "Sparkles, I'd like you to formally meet your friend Rayline. We call her Sunshine."

"Or Junior," I quipped.

"Don't ruin the introductions," my brother complained. "Sunshine, this is Sparkles."

Matt and my niece stayed in the barn until Rayline created a smelly reason for him to return to the house to change her diaper. Left alone, I talked to the unicorn by myself.

I detected Mason's presence before he spoke. "You here to check in on me, too?"

"No. I came over to see you and ran into your brother. He told me where you were."

"Tattletale," I murmured with a sigh, pushing off the fence of the stall.

Mason joined me in watching the unicorn. "He also told me you'd come up with a name. Rainbow Sparkles?"

"Just Sparkles. If you stand here long enough, you might find out how we came up with the moniker." The image of the unicorn raising her tail and aiming her behind at the detective tickled me, and I giggled.

"What's so funny?" Mason asked.

"Stand here long enough and you might find out," I repeated, snickering. "Why were you coming over to see me if you weren't checking on me."

The detective breathed out a long sigh. "Fine. Maybe I was. But I had something else I wanted to talk to you about."

I ruffled Sparkles' mane, focusing on her instead of the butterflies flitting around in my stomach. "Go ahead."

"This might sound crazy, but ever since we came back from Charleston, I've been having odd dreams," he started.

"Like what?" I pressed.

"Well, in most, I'm flying through the air."

"That's not that strange. You are an expert in flying a broom." Something I'd been adamant I wouldn't do again anytime soon.

He rubbed the back of his neck. "Yeah, but when I'm flying, I'm not alone."

Chills ran down my body and the hair on my arms stood up. "Mm-hmm?"

Mason took a beat before continuing. "I'm sure that it's you who's sitting in front of me. I have my arms wrapped around to hold onto the handle in front of you."

My breath hitched. The detective wasn't dreaming. He was remembering.

"And that's all you dream about? Flying on a broom with me?" I didn't want to push him too hard for fear it might shatter the tiny bubble of hope growing in my chest.

"No." Mason placed his warm hand over mine. "The visions of flying remain, but I see more than just where we're headed. I see things that can't come from me. They're from you. Like knowing how it was for you growing up in your family. And experiencing what it's like when you work your magic."

A squeal of excitement rose in my throat, but I choked it down. "That sounds different, but not odd."

"Why?" he asked. "I know you know the answer."

I allowed myself to look at him. His eyes pleaded with me to tell him the truth. "Because those aren't dreams. They're your memories. We flew together several times on your broom. And while we did, we shared our magic, which allowed barriers between us to break. You shared some of your experiences with me as I did with you. Out of all the people in the world, you were the one who understood me fully. Until..."

"Until my memories of you were stripped from me," Mason finished. "And after our visit to the Angel Oak, they're coming back?"

I opened my mouth to tell him yes but lacked the confidence to know for certain. "I can't promise that."

He squeezed my hand and let go. "I know. But whether or not I'll recover whatever happened between us or if it only comes in my dreams, I know that whatever exists between us," Mason turned to face me, "I'm not afraid of it."

"Really?" I took a step back. "Because, sweet honeysuckle iced tea, I sure am."

A barrage of questions flooded into my head. What if he remembered but he'd changed his mind? What if he never remembered and we just remained friends? Too many *what if's* clouded my vision until he reached out and brushed my hair away from my face.

"Charli," he uttered, cradling my face. "Be scared if you want. I'll be brave for both of us." He leaned closer until his breath blew across my skin.

My eyes fluttered in anticipation, and I started to close them until the unicorn nickered and raised its tail.

"Oh, no." Despite knowing what was coming, I couldn't stop watching.

With an undignified sound, a glittering rainbow cloud erupted from the creature's behind, ruining Mason's and my moment.

"Huh. Sparkles. Now I get the name." He sighed and placed his forehead against mine, stroking my cheek with his thumb. "To be continued," he breathed out.

"Let's go inside and I'll pour you some sweet tea," I offered, gripping his hand in mine.

"Lead the way."

We left Sparkles with waves and promises to return. The afternoon sun warmed me, but not as much as the hope of combining the past and the present with Mason did. There was still a lot of healing left, and I couldn't predict where we'd end up.

On my way to the house, I couldn't help but think about Abigail. I'd waited to hear from her that she was okay. Every day, I checked my mailbox and searched around my house for a hidden note. Once I got ahold of her address, I could mail her the gifts I'd bought at the market in Charleston as a reminder of what we'd started together. In another week or so, I would enlist everyone's help to try and track her down if she didn't send me word.

Our first meeting hadn't gone well, but I knew in my gut we'd see each other again. Her willing sacrifice to try and keep me away from whatever problems she knew my blood relatives could bring to me, she'd earned her spot in my chosen family. And as my family, I would risk a lot to protect her. Even if that meant I cut out the rest of those related to me by blood.

While Mason and I drank sweet tea and rocked on my porch in companionable silence with Biddy and Peaches in our midst, it felt like both of us waited at a crossroads to find out which way things would turn. As Mama Lee said, what fun would life be without a few surprises? I hoped the detective would be a part of at least some of them in my future.

"Are we good?" he asked between creaks of our rocking chairs.

I smiled and gazed out at the horizon. "We will be."

Dear Reader -

Thanks so much for reading *Barbecue & Brooms*! If you enjoyed the book (as much as I did writing it), I hope you'll consider leaving a review!

Cornbread & Crossroads will be available soon! Sign up for my newsletter to find out when it's out!

NEWSLETTER ONLY - If you want to be notified when the next story is released and to get access to exclusive content, sign up for my newsletter! https://www.subscribepage.com/t4v5z6

NEWSLETTER & FREE PREQUEL - to gain exclusive access to the prequel *Chess Pie & Choices*, go here! https://dl.bookfunnel.com/opbg5ghpyb

Southern Charms Cozy Mystery Series

Magic and mystery are only part of the Southern Charms of Honeysuckle Hollow...

Suggested reading order:

Chess Pie & Choices: Prequel

Moonshine & Magic: Book 1

Lemonade & Love Potions: A Cozy Short

Fried Chicken & Fangs: Book 2

Sweet Tea & Spells: Book 3

Barbecue & Brooms: Book 4

Collards & Cauldrons: Book 5

Cornbread & Crossroads: Book 6 (Coming Soon)

Join my reader group:

www.facebook.com/groups/southerncharmscozycompanions/

Southern Relics Cozy Mysteries

Sign up for the Newsletter to hear when the new series is released! https://www.subscribepage.com/t4v5z6

Flea Market Magic: Book 1
Rags to Witches: Book 2
Pickups and Pirates: Book 3

Sassy witch, Ruby Mae Jewell, uses her savvy know-how to find a good bargain and her elemental magic of fire to search for objects and relics imbued with magical powers to keep them out of mortal hands. Of course, in her quests, she faces murders, mysteries, and mayhem!

Acknowledgments

I usually save thanking my supportive husband until the very end, but for this book, I want to put him front and center. I truly appreciate the encouragement and patience you give to allow me to live out my dream. You deserve many home cooked meals to make up for the nights you have to eat leftovers.

To my group of writer friends who are located far and wide: thanks for getting together in person once in a while and reminding me that having a community is what makes us better!

Special thanks go to my plot sisters, Danielle Garrett and Melanie Summers, who gave up lots of their time to help me work through my story, and to my other coffee coven members, Tegan Maher and Cate Lawley for pushing me with writing sprints.

And finally, a big thank you to my readers, especially my reader group members, the Southern Charmers! Not only do you help me do cool things like name unicorns but you also make sure to keep me on track and ready to share more stories with you. Thanks for reading!

About the Author

Bella Falls grew up on the magic of sweet tea, barbecue, and hot and humid Southern days. She met her husband at college over an argument of how to properly pronounce the word *pecan* (for the record, it should be *pea-cawn,* and they taste amazing in a pie). Although she's had the privilege of living all over the States and the world, her heart still beats to the rhythm of the cicadas on a hot summer's evening.

Now, she's taken her love of the South and woven it into a world where magic and mystery aren't the only Charms.

bellafallsbooks.com
contact@bellafallsbooks.com
https://www.facebook.com/
groups/southerncharmscozycompanions/

facebook.com/bellafallsbooks

twitter.com/bellafallsbooks

instagram.com/bellafallsbooks

amazon.com/author/bellafalls

Made in the USA
Monee, IL
18 May 2021